THE MONTANA BADMEN

'Let the rope twang!' was the motto of the Montana vigilantes when their untamed territory was the scene of thuggery, killing and lawlessness. Battle-weary Shoot Johannson was heading for Virginia City to seek his fortune in the goldfields. However, when he falls for the sultry-eyed Susan he is soon involved in another world of violent intrigue. Is the town marshal, Henry Plummer, behind the gang preying on stagecoach bullion convoys? Whose side is Susan on? Shoot strongly resists joining in lynch law, but as bullying and back-stabbing accelerate, he too is forced to resort to the rope and the gun.

THE MONTANA BADMEN

THE MONTANA BADMEN

by

John Dyson

Dales Large Print Books
Long Preston, North Yorkshire,
BD23 4ND, England.

British Library Cataloguing in Publication Data.

Dyson, John
The Montana badmen.

A catalogue record of this book is
available from the British Library

ISBN 1-84262-210-2 pbk

First published in Great Britain in 1995 by Robert Hale Limited

Published in Large Print 2002 by arrangement with
Robert Hale Limited

Dales Large Print is an imprint of Library Magna Books Ltd.

Printed and bound in Great Britain by
T.J. (International) Ltd., Cornwall, PL28 8RW

ONE

The Oregon mule-packer was eyeing the Sharps carbine laid over Shoot Johannson's knees. 'You know how to use that weapon, son?'

'Should do. I lost count of the men I killed the past two years.'

'Who you kiddin'? Don't give me that bull. You ain't old enough.'

'I'm old enough.' There was a bitter tone to Shoot's voice as he remembered the friends and enemies slaughtered, the horror and the fear of two years of war. 'Joined the 1st US Sharpshooters in '61 when I was sixteen. Was at Bull Run when the Rebs ran us all the way back to Washington. I was at Antietam and Fredericksburg. Sure, I'm old enough.'

Shoot was sitting on a barrel outside the agency trading store on the Nez Perce reservation. He was a slim, broad-shouldered young man with a slab of pale hair falling across his brow. A Colt Navy revolver was stashed in his belt and he wore the collar of his reefer jacket pulled up against a cold wind that blew down from the icy peaks of the Rockies.

'In that case whatcha doin' in Idaho?'

Shoot watched the burly packer in his lumber-jack clothes as he busied himself harnessing a team of twenty mules. He guessed it wouldn't do any harm to tell him. He had escaped from the horror of all that war back there, even if he would never escape the shock, the trauma and nightmares. It wasn't likely out here in the wilderness that he would run into a Union officer who would put him up against a wall and shoot him as a deserter.

'You know,' he said, 'of the fifteen hundred brave boys I joined my regiment with in New York there's only five hundred left. And we weren't the gunfodder. We were the skirmishers and snipers. Guess you could say I took French leave.'

The packer kicked a knee into the gut of his ornery lead mule and jerked her cinch tighter. 'You ain't the only one,' he grunted. 'Hear say there's thousands desertin'. Most of the men out here are on the lam from somethun'.'

The packer had brought government supplies of flour and blankets up the Columbia river from Portland, along the Snake confluent and up the Clearwater to the reservation. He was on his way back with pelts traded with trappers and Indians.

'So you're heading across the mountains into Montana to seek your fortune?'

'Guess I got as good a chance as any man.'

'Well, you sure gonna need that carbine.'

'Why so? Trouble with Indians?'

'It ain't the Injins I was thinkin' of. These Nez Perce are friendly enough. And the Bannacks have had most of the fight whipped out of 'em, although you never know. Them and the Sioux are gittin' riled up 'cause of the Bozeman Trail pushing through their huntin' grounds. No, I was thinking of scurvy sonuvabitch white men.'

'Why's that?'

'Montana Territory's infested with desperadoes. Rattlesnake, Cottonwood, Bannack and Virginia City, there's shootings every day. These men don't kill for anger or greed but jest for the fun of it. They prey on travellers. They seem to know every time a big consignment of gold's being taken out, or a miner's got dust in his pockets. Not many get through.'

'Hey, you trying to scare me?' Shoot grinned as he slung his tarp sack of supplies and a few belongings across the neck of the bobtailed piebald he had bought from a Nez Perce brave for ten dollars. They were the first Indians he had encountered and, even if they didn't have pierced noses, they were a handsome, arrogant race in their feathers and beaded buckskins. Once they had been lords of this beautiful land of rivers, lakes, woods and mountains. Now they were the underdogs, but they still looked as if they reckoned themselves a cut above the white man. 'I'm hopeful this nag will get me to where I'm going.'

'You was robbed.' The packer laughed, showing his broken teeth. 'Hey, hold on to this rope, will ya.'

Shoot walked over. The lead mule's eyes rolled and she lashed out with her hind foot. Shoot felt the breeze pass his knee as he jumped back. The packer smashed a fist into the mule's jaw, making her shudder. 'Not so close. Millie could cripple ya. She knows better not to try it with me.'

'Which do you reckon's my best route to Montana?'

The packer pointed to the distant white fangs of a mountain range. 'Go south-east across the high plain. Sooner or later you'll strike the trail that cuts through the Big

Divide' – he laughed again – 'if you're lucky.'

'Well, I've come all this way, I ain't giving up now.'

When he had walked out of the army and back home to New York, he had said goodbye to his folks and signed on before the mast on a windjammer, 10,000 miles around Cape Horn. A three months voyage. At San Francisco he had jumped ship, worked his passage on a steam-sail up to the Columbia. And on along the Oregon Trail. A long journey but he had made it.

'Where's the ramrod on this thang?' The muleskinner had finished his packing and was taking a look at the Sharps.

'There ain't. It's a breechloader. The days of the old muzzleloader are numbered. I paid seventy dollars for it in Frisco. This year's model, a '63. The latest state of the art.'

'Give me my ole Kentucky any day.' The packer squinted along the sights. 'Cain't be very accurate with this titchy barrel. What did ya have to do to git into them Sharp-shooters?'

'Get ten shots from a rifle in a ten-inch circle from two hundred yards. That was the official army test. Cain't say I could do it with a carbine, but the shorter barrel sure makes it easier to handle on horseback.'

A commotion was coming from down at the river where Indian women and children were being ducked under the water by a man wearing a top hat and frock coat.

'What's goin' on?'

'Ach!' The packer spat and tossed the Sharps back to Shoot. 'Some sonuvabitch missionary is baptizing 'em Christians. Them Nez Perces think they'll get better land and supplies if they see the light. And maybe they will. If you ask me it's only gonna cause trouble between the tribes. There's no way Chief Joseph will give up his old religion. That interferin' preacher oughta be sent scuttlin'.'

Shoot spread his blanket on the horse's back as a saddle and jumped aboard. 'How many yards you reckon that is, a hundred?' He grinned at the packer, pulled his new plainsman's wide-brimmed hat down over his eyes, the carbine into his shoulder, aimed carefully and squeezed the trigger. As the shot cracked out the preacher's silk hat was whipped from his head into the water.

'How about that?' Shoot tugged at the piebald's bridle, whirling her around. 'Tell him I'll buy him a new hat in Virginny City.'

‘Stay outa trouble, son.’

‘That’s the last thing I want.’

Shoot kicked in his heels and sent the bobtail spurting away, out across the emptiness of the high plains, out towards the mountains. He took his directions from a rough map he had copied out at the agency. At first the wagon trail was plain enough, but after he had passed small farmsteads and reached open country the track began to fade into the prairie. And then it took a fork nobody had told him about. Shoot decided to take the left-hand branch.

For days he did not see a soul but jogged on his way, heading towards a range of mountains that reared their jagged heads. They must, he reckoned, be the Bitteroots. The nearer he got the more harsh and imposing they seemed, their pinnacles covered with snow. Somehow he had to get through them, but he wasn’t sure how. None of the landmarks he had been looking out for had appeared. He felt like a mariner adrift in the ocean in a small boat. ‘Let’s face it,’ he muttered, as dusk began to fall on the sixth night and he stopped to make camp. ‘I’m completely lost. Don’t you know the way, hoss?’

The air was breathtakingly chilly at this altitude, and there were still patches of snow about. Shoot spent a miserable night huddled in his sleeping bag; in spite of pulling his sailor's sock-cap down over his ears, and his hat on top of that, an insistent drizzle dripped down his neck.

In the morning his horse had disappeared.

'Shee-it!' he said, as he tried to light a fire with damp wood. 'I knew I shoulda tied up that nag. I guess she's gotten more sense than me and gone home.'

He couldn't get the fire to light and had to make do for breakfast with a swig of cold water and a mouthful of damp yesterday's flapjack and set off on foot to look for the pony. His worn boots had sprung a leak and his feet were cold and damp as he squelched across a sodden terrain of grass and rocks that seemed to stretch on into an eternity of distance. The sense of space awed him. And there was no sign of the horse.

'This is stupid,' he said. He guessed he would just have to head on across the plain and try to climb over the mountains. He walked on under a grey louring sky, his tarpaulin pack over his shoulder and carbine in his hand. On and on he walked. Until, suddenly, he saw a movement in the distance. He stopped, frozen in his tracks, and gradually crouched down. A band of riders! And they had feathers in their hair!

The saliva in Shoot's mouth seemed to go dry. His heart began thumping hard. Harder. These didn't look like Nez Perce or Shoshones. They were bare-legged and bare-chested red men. They looked much more wild.

Shoot reckoned he had as much courage as any other young fellow. He had done his patriotic duty and volunteered. He had gone through fire and bloodshed. He had charged when the sergeant told him to charge, as his comrades fell around him, and cannon shot cut men and trees to stumps. He had campaigned through winter when mules were up to their ears in mud. He had fought until he was sickened by the foolishness and futility of it all. And then, like thousands of others, he had deserted and made his way back to New York. He had signed on before the mast and hadn't whinged too much when he was whipped up into the windjammer's great masts to reef sails in a horrendous gale. He had acquitted himself well against river thieves. But this time he was scared. Real scared.

Shoot wriggled away uphill on his belly

through the damp grass. He found a hidey-hole in a clump of rocks, hurriedly prepared his charges, and held the Sharps in readiness, squinting out through a crack in the boulders. His only hope was that the Indians wouldn't find his tracks. He reminded himself to keep his last shot for himself. He had heard too many tales of how an Indian delighted in slowly torturing a man to death. Surely he hadn't come all this way for that?

The band of Indians drew level in his sights. They were not wearing war paint, but they looked a vicious crew. They were carrying bows and feathered coup sticks and had one side of the head shaved. They were talking animatedly among themselves and pointing to the ground. One of them was leading Shoot's piebald.

The best defence, Shoot had been told, was to attack. Maybe he could kill two or three of them, maybe scare them off? His finger squeezed the trigger half-to. Yes, they had seen his tracks. They were turning towards his rocks. Maybe he should use his revolver? If they all charged together it would give him more chance. In a panic of indecision he put the Sharps aside, pulled the revolver out, cocked it with his thumb.

They were getting closer, climbing their horses up towards him. It was now or...

The leading Indian had halted. He seemed to be sniffing the air, as if he had scented a white man. His nostrils quivered with disgust. And he raised one hand, either to halt his men, or, could it mean peace? Was it a trick?

Shoot knew they knew where he was. He hesitated a moment, and rose to his feet. He raised his open left hand, keeping his revolver in his right hand cocked.

The Indians looked surprised. One of them raised his lance as if to throw but held it poised.

'I am friend,' Shoot called, and felt foolish and exposed. He knew they could kill him if they so chose. For seconds it was as if he was suspended between life and death.

'That's my horse.' He stepped out of the rocks, walked towards them with a bluff of authority.

They spoke words he didn't understand. He put his revolver back in his belt to show he did not want to harm them. There wasn't much he could do now. He pointed to the horse and back to his chest. 'Horse. Mine. I bought.'

Again they chattered among themselves,

pointing to him and to the horse. The leader leapt down to stand before Shoot, his legs apart. 'Where – you – go?' He prodded his finger at Shoot's chest as he said each word.

'Bannack City.' Shoot pointed over the mountain range, and added, weakly, 'I guess I'm kinda lost.'

'He – lost.' The Indian's savage demeanour split into a grin, and the rest of them began to laugh. 'Me Bannack.' The Indian waved his hands at the prairie. 'Bannack land. You no cross.'

Shoot thought for a moment. What could he lose? He went back to the rocks, picked up his Sharps, and turned to them. 'You take me to Bannack City' – he tried to indicate by signs what he meant – 'I give you gun. Good gun. The best. Cost me many dollars. Good for hunting.'

The leader stepped forward, took the carbine from him, but not with undue force. He examined it, curiously, turned and aimed at a boulder. The horses jumped away as the explosion startled them, and the boulder was chipped. 'Good,' the Indian said. 'More shot. You show me.'

'I show you at Bannack City.' Shoot brandished the bag of shot, touched his chest and his lips (he had an idea that showed he was speaking the truth). 'You lead me.'

He guessed they could just ride off with the carbine if they so chose. Or force him to show them how to put the charges in. They had ways ... but, after some chattering, the leading Indian handed the gun back. He took the piebald's halter from one of his men and passed it to Shoot.

'You. Me. Bannack City,' he said, his dark eyes on Shoot. 'Bannack City. Me. Gun.'

Shoot put his hand out to shake on the deal, and the red man clutched his wrist with a wide smile.

The other Bannacks laughed and insisted on shaking hands with him, too, before they gave shrill whoops and cantered away across the plain.

Shoot grabbed his blanket and pack and jumped on to the pony. 'Come,' the Bannack said, and knee'd his horse in a southerly direction. It didn't seem right to Shoot, but he guessed he had to trust him. He went jogging after the Indian.

As they went south they climbed their ponies up into the mountains, up through a dense dark brush of conifers. The Bannack appeared to know an almost invisible path, a mere deer trail, but which eventually brought them above the treeline to a region of harsh mossy rock. Before leaving the woods, to Shoot's puzzlement, the Indian roped a small dead fir and dragged it along behind him. On they climbed, all day, higher into the great chasms, until they reached the beginning of the snowline. It was too precipitous to ride, so they led their ponies, which scrambled after them, agile as goats. It must have been mid-afternoon when the blizzard came down and they were engulfed in a white-out. On and up the Bannack climbed, and Shoot stumbled after him, trying to keep in sight the Indian's dark, muscular bare legs, fearing that he would disappear into the blinding flakes.

The wind shrieked and tugged at his clothing and his hat like witches trying to pull him from the precarious path. He pulled his piebald onwards, his boots slipping, the flying snow congealing his eyes, scrabbling up after the Indian, his pony and the towed tree. Suddenly the blizzard ceased, the mist of clouds cleared, and Shoot looked out over a vast chasm at a great hulking mountain, its walls as smooth and white as glass, and down, thousands of feet below, to a silver stream winding across the prairie.

He looked up and saw the narrow defile the Indian was following. Tongues of snow trickled down the dark exposed rock towards them, as if warning them not to dare go further. His lungs were being pierced by arrows of ice. The wind howled with laughter and the blizzard hit them with renewed force, wiping out visibility beyond ten feet. Surely it was madness to go on?

But the Bannack had disappeared up the slope, so Shoot hurried after him. One false step and he knew he could go tumbling over that precipice out into space.

When it grew dark the Bannack beckoned him into the shelter of an overhanging rock. Shoot saw now why he had brought the tree: for firewood. The Bannack broke it up with his tomahawk, hunkered down and soon had a fire going. Shoot used snow to make dough of his flour. He rolled it into strips and wound it round his carbine barrel like he had done in the army. He cooked it in the flames and offered the first strip to the red man. He sliced off a hunk of frozen bacon and roasted it on his knife point, handing a piece over. He watched the dark, aquiline features of the Bannack as he chewed, the intermeshing of the jawbones, the half-shaven scalp, the solemn eyes in the firelight. The Indian gave a grunt of appreciation as he squatted in his blanket. Shoot, too, felt better with something in his stomach, although the wind was trickling freezing fingers about his back, making his body shudder. He crushed coffee beans with his carbine butt and boiled up snow in his billy can. He shared a scalding cupful with his new *amigo*, and smiled to see their shadows against the half-cave wall. One dark silhouette feathered, the other behatted!

But it was too cold to talk. They tethered the ponies with lariats. The poor sturdy creatures pawed at the snow but there was little vegetation for them to crop. The Indian rolled his blanket around him and Shoot crawled into his bag. They lay almost on top of the blaze. Shoot pulled his wool hat over his nose and tried to sleep. At first he kept his revolver between his knees. And then he pushed it down beneath his toes. They said you could never trust an Indian. But this one, he knew, was as honest as a rock.

It was a long cold night. But the dawn always comes, and when it did it was a magnificent sight. The blizzard had ceased. Before them stretched the icy peaks of the

Continental Divide, glowing incarnadine in the rays of the rising sun. It was a sight breathtaking and magical. They were high on one of the ranges of the Rockies, on a northern part of that spinal chain that runs down through the Americas, the southern tip of which Shoot had glimpsed as his ship ploughed through the Magellan Straits.

He pulled on his boots, trying to cease from shivering, marvelling at how his half-naked companion seemed almost immune to cold. They hurried on across the ridge and went slipping and sliding down the other side. Shoot felt lightheaded. He wanted to yell for joy. He was almost disappointed when they reached the treeline once more.

'Bannack City,' the Bannock said, pointing along a green and grey valley. 'Bad people. Me no go.'

'How far?'

'One' – he made a hands-pointed sign for sleep – 'you there. Many bad men.' He gave a look of disgust. 'Me no like.'

'Fair enough,' Shoot said, and took the seventy-dollar carbine from his shoulder. He found the bag of shot and showed the Indian how to reload. As he did so a delicately limbed young doe stepped out of the wood fifty yards away. 'Look,' he whispered. He fired, and the creature collapsed, shot through the heart behind its front leg.

Shoot gave a whoop. 'Time for breakfast. Or maybe brunch.'

The Bannack deftly skinned and gutted the deer, rolling up the hide and hiding the innards behind a rock. They made a fire and roasted a hind leg. The flesh was tender and delicious. After filling their bellies they lay back in the bracken and watched the ponies cropping shoots.

'I heard somewhere that an Indian doesn't like being asked his name, sort of discourteous, but my name's Shoot. Me' – he tapped his chest – 'Shoot.'

'Shoot?'

'Yes. My name.'

The Bannack's face suddenly lit with understanding. 'Me. Five Owls.'

'Five Owls. That's good. A wise name. You're a wise man. You know the mountain paths.'

'Yes. Me know good.'

Shoot jumped up and handed him the carbine. 'It's yours. And take the rest of the deer. Yes, go on. I'll be heading on.'

He swung on to his piebald and leaned

across to shake the Bannack's hand once more. 'So long, Five Owls. And thanks. Good hunting!'

He kicked his heels into the piebald and set her at a canter down towards the valley. When he reached the flat he turned and looked back at the dark conifers. The Bannack had disappeared.

TWO

The icy peaks of the Rockies were flushed pale pink. The glimmering sun, low in the sky, westered. The only sounds Shoot heard were the harsh breathing of his mount as she plodded on across the green and watery plain, and the suction as her hoofs sank into the marshy ground. The wind had ceased and the air was strangely still and clear. The grass had a lush greenness, the scattered rocks a harsh greyness, and the lakes of floodwater shone like bright silver. Spring came late in these northern parts, and at this high altitude, but the snows were finally melting. If he had thought about it Shoot would have agreed that the scene before him had much melancholy grandeur. But he wasn't thinking about scenery. He was wondering how much longer it would take to get to the mountain backwater of Bannack City. And what he would do when he got there.

Gold by the bucketful was being dug out of the gulches back of the city or so he had heard. This was the scene of the latest 'stampede', as they called it, or gold rush. Shoot was a little laggard in getting there. By this time, in early '63, there were already thousands of miners, traders and their inevitable hangers-on dug in in the mountains. Most probably all the best claims had been cleaned out by now.

It was good to see signs of white folk once more for the first time since leaving the Snake River. As he rode along the valley he passed bleak farmsteads built of logs with sod roofs, pole corrals for cattle, haggard men behind oxen and plough trying to bust the hostile soil. He had to admit they looked none too friendly, and Shoot went loping past on his way.

Hoving up on the horizon however, he spied a collection of low, timber dwellings that had all the appearances of a town. Could this be Bannack? No, there was no signs of mining. It was getting late. Maybe he should stay the night?

'Bear Paw' a crudely painted sign said, and underneath, 'Pop: 75', which had been crossed out to read, '73'. They must have had a couple of deaths recently. It was a dismal place, a few dilapidated stores lining a wide muddy main street. 'Liquors and cigars', one boasted. Another more mundanely offered, 'Flour, nails, tools, and oil'. There was a drab lodging house and a couple of barns. And a saloon, through the murky windows of which, Shoot, as he plodded past, could see the dark figures of a few men sprawled about tables in the glow of a hurricane lamp.

'What a Godforsaken hole,' he muttered to the piebald. 'Maybe we'll just buy a few supplies and head on.'

The pony didn't seem to think much of this idea. She gave a spluttering snort and shook her head. Shoot guessed she felt she was due a night in the warm straw of a livery. 'Well, you've brought me this far. Maybe you're right.' He wouldn't be averse to a night in a proper bed, either, instead of sleeping out in the foul weather under some rock at the mercy of – who knew – any more wandering Indians. They were supposed to be at peace, but in September similarly peaceful Santée Sioux in Minnesota Territory had risen up in a frenzy of blood-letting that had left 800 settlers slaughtered in one month. Here in Montana the Shoshone were getting increasingly agitated about the stampede of prospectors across their tribal lands in breach of their treaties. Maybe, like those Bannacks, they were too much in awe of the white man to cause trouble. But a man couldn't count on it.

'Heck,' Shoot said. 'I've convinced myself. This sure ain't the safest territory for a man to be riding through alone.

He climbed down, hitched the horse, and opened a rattling door to a dimly lit store. He made purchases of coffee, hard biscuits, matches, and barley sugar, as the sour-faced woman behind the counter eyed him with what could only be called apprehension. 'Am I on the right trail for Bannack City, ma'am?'

She nodded, pushed him to the door with his groceries and pointed towards the mountains. 'Jest keep on going,' she croaked. 'An' if you've any sense you'll go now.'

'Why's that?' Shoot asked, but by that time she had slammed the door shut, locked it, and was busy putting up the shutters.

He cracked off a mouthful of barley sugar and stowed his purchases in his bags. The sun gave one last faint glimmer and disappeared behind a hill as a melancholy dusk descended over the houses. Shoot left his pony in the livery and paid out two dollars for the night. 'What's going on?' Shoot asked the ostler. 'Why's everybody look so shit-scared?'

The man spat into the straw and muttered, 'You'll maybe find out.' He, too, locked up the stable doors and hurried away into the gloom.

Shoot scratched himself and thought of taking a nice hot bath in the barber shop. As he went to enter, a fat, bald-headed man turned the sign around to 'Closed'. He peered through the glass and beckoned him urgently away.

'A real friendly neighbourhood,' Shoot said. 'This place sure gives me the creeps.'

He looked across at the saloon and saw some surly-faced men peering out of the window at him. First I gotta find a place to stay, he thought. He trudged through the mud along to the lodging house. Another muddy-faced shrew opened her door to him an inch, peeped out, and hissed, 'Yes, what do you want?'

'A bed for the night, ma'am, if you have one.'

She looked doubtful, but came out and ushered him around the back to a built-on cabin. The shutters had already been put up. It was dark, damp and musty, but there was a cot and a couple of blankets and a lamp. 'Do you do food?' he asked, paying her a dollar.

'No. I wasn't expecting nobody. Maybe over at the saloon. You want to be quick about it. If I were you, young man, I wouldn't bother. You'd be best advised to lock your door, douse your lamp and get to bed. You can always eat in the morning.'

'Why? What's going on?'

'You'd be ill-advised to stay out late. Don't say I haven't warned you.' She hurried back into her wooden house, slamming the door.

Funny woman, Shoot thought. He made sure his eight-inch-barrelled revolver was securely tucked into the stout leather belt round his waist. He hitched up his trousers with their reinforced leather patches, and frayed bottoms, and buttoned his seaman's reefer jacket to conceal the weapon. He pulled down his new hat and, pushing out his broad chest, strode over to the saloon.

'Good evening, gentlemen,' he said, as he entered, blowing on his fingers to warm them, and stamping some life into his feet in his damp and leaky boots.

None of the men answered him. They looked like swarthy mongrel dogs in their dirty farm clothes and beards. There was a mix of fear and resentment in their eyes. 'Whadja want?' the man standing behind the bar asked.

'A glass of rum to warm me. And maybe some vittles, if you have any.'

The landlord was an unsavoury individual, skinny, bony-nosed, greasy strands of hair plastered over his brow. He wore a crumpled suit that looked like he generally slept in it, and a dirty collarless shirt. He filled a tumbler with rum without a word and thumped it down before the young stranger. 'All we got's bread and cheese.'

'That'll do me fine.'

The man eyed him. 'You one of the captain's men?'

'The captain? Who's he?'

'One of the richest men in the Territory,' a voice growled behind him. 'And one of the worst.'

'No,' Shoot said, turning to the speaker. 'I'm just a traveller. Headin' for Bannack City to try my luck.'

'Huh! You're lucky you're not headin' away with a poke of gold dust. You wouldn't have it long, not in these parts.'

'There's not many who strike it lucky get back alive,' another chimed in.

'Jesus!' Shoot took a gulp of the musty liquid and blinked as it burned his throat. 'Seems like I'm in for a cheerful evening.'

The seven occupants of the bar relapsed

into a sullen silence, huddled in their worn coats, their boots stuck out, staring through the cobwebbed window at the settling dusk.

'Well, I'm not hanging around to face them,' one suddenly said, jumping up. 'I'm off back to my farm.'

'I thought you were going to all stick by me,' the landlord whined. 'That's right. Scuttle off.'

'I've a wife and children to think of,' the man said, as he hurried out. 'I'm not a fighting man.'

'None of us are,' one of the men commented, miserably.

'You expecting trouble?' Shoot pressed.

'You could put it like that.'

'Who is this captain?'

'Captain James Slade, a fine, upstanding gentleman, when he's sober,' the landlord intoned, bitterly. 'But when he's on a whiskey jag he becomes the very devil out of hell.'

'I see,' Shoot said.

'He killed two men last week. Or his men did. Forced them into a quarrel. And we have information he's headed this way again tonight.'

'Jesus have mercy on us,' another man whispered.

'Aren't you going to fight him?'

'Fight!' one of the men screamed. 'He would burn us to the ground.'

'I see,' Shoot repeated, and thought, I had a feeling I ought to have kept going tonight.

He had finished the bread and cheese and pickles, and another glass of rum, and decided it might be a good idea to have an early night when he heard the sound of gunfire. Three riders came charging into the main street of Bear Paw, shooting off their six-guns and yelling like Indians. They careered up and down the street a couple of times, jumped from their mustangs, and lurched unsteadily into the bar.

'Ah, my fine feathered friends. This is where you have been hiding.' The speaker doffed his slouch hat in mockery. He was a middle-aged man, not unhandsome, if of florid complexion, his voice a deep, slurred, cultivated drawl. He had a neatly clipped moustache and a military air, and gave a great roar of laughter. 'Set up the whiskey, Ephraim.'

The landlord opened his mouth but no words came out. He glanced at the others, braced himself, and said, 'I'm sorry, Captain. I can't serve you. Not after the trouble we had last time. You've already had a good drop. We, us citizens of Bear Paw, we're all agreed. We would ask you politely, sir, to ride on.'

'You, *what?*' Captain Slade hammered his fist on to the bar making the timbers shake. 'Look at them, boys. What a miserable, bedraggled coop of chickens they are. And they don't like us in their roost.'

'It's no use being nasty, Captain. We don't want no trouble, that's all.'

'You–' The captain seemed lost for words. He stood there in his heavy Union greatcoat and high boots, between his two companions, hard-looking men dressed like ranch hands, but heavily laden with guns.

One, in his early twenties, stomped and roared, cursing the landlord, the other men, as sons-of-bitches and worse. Bull-necked and ugly, his tufty hair looked as if it had been self-cropped with sheep-shears to save a dollar, and his complexion was red-raw, either from the cold or too close a shave. A bully, braggart, loudmouth and yahoo, in short. 'Hell take you,' he shouted, and swaggered around the bar, pushing the landlord out of his way. He grabbed a bottle of whiskey from the shelf and crashed it down. 'There you are, Captain.'

'Jem, Jem, you are indeed a gem,' Slade

smiled, and poured three large tumblers with a shaky hand. He lifted one, swallowed it in two gulps, and poured more. His two sidekicks sipped theirs with more respect for the gut-churning sourmash. They stood there talking, ignoring the onlookers as they got through the bottle. 'Damned impertinence,' the captain said. 'The money I give the traders of this town. And that's their gratitude.'

'Have it your own way, Captain,' the landlord cried. 'That's finest Kentucky whiskey. Five dollars a bottle.'

Jem snatched up the bottle and gave him a backhander across the bridge of his nose with it, felling him. The landlord crawled into a corner clutching at a bloody eye.

'Ephraim!' the captain tut-tutted. 'You poor fool. You should know better than to interrupt us when we're drinking. I could buy you out tomorrow if I cared to. I could buy this whole damned useless town.'

'Not my eye,' Ephraim moaned. 'You needn't have done my eye.'

A man sitting beside Shoot gave an audible sigh. 'Here goes,' he murmured. He was a stocky, stubby-nosed Irishman, who appeared to have a bit more backbone than the others.

'Did somebody say something?' The other thug, a week's growth of beard on his long face, his tall hat pulled down over his eyes, turned to them, his eyes gleaming threateningly, his fingers brushing the butt of his revolver.

'You cannot be taunting us to draw,' Shoot's neighbour said, a burr to his words. 'We are not armed. Or maybe that don't worry scum like you?'

'Why, you–'

'Boon, leave him,' the captain said, catching at the gunman's elbow. 'Don't do him the favour. For from now on he would be better off dead. Mark him. He'll be sorry for those words.' He looked at the broken bottle and shook his head. 'Jem, Jem, my boy. You shouldn't have done that. Such a waste of whiskey.'

'There's plenty more, Cap.' The cowhand behind the bar gave a whoop and grabbed another bottle, kicking out at Ephraim, who was grovelling on the floor trying to get up. 'I'll close the other eye if he ain't careful.'

'Ingratitude, Ephraim,' the captain whispered, opening the new bottle. 'You've cut me to the quick.' He turned to the watchers. 'Don't I always pay my debts? Don't I reimburse you for any damage when the boys and I are having a bit of fun?'

'That's not the point,' the man beside Shoot said. 'It's the outrage. You treat us like dogs, sir. There's no need to do that to poor Ephraim. He's only running his business.'

'Shut your trap, bogman.' The long-jawed man's eyes were as cold as death as they flickered over them. 'Who's your friend? I ain't seen him before.'

'Maybe I've only got a small spread and you're the biggest rancher in the valley, Captain, but it don't give you the right to come stomping in here like this.'

'Stomping in here?' the captain protested. 'I was making a quiet social call when that, that filth down there, insulted me.'

'I asked who your friend was,' the long-faced man said, pulling his jacket aside to clear his revolver.

'I'm not his friend,' Shoot said. 'I'm just passing through.'

'The hell you are,' the man snarled. 'Nobody's going nowhere unless we say so.'

'True. You can't trust these bastards,' the captain shouted, swaying drunkenly. 'Telling me he can't serve me.'

Shoot got to his feet and went to push his way past out of the bar. 'Goodnight, gents,' he said.

A fist with a revolver in it shot out and into his solar plexus. A rivetting pain hit him as he gasped for air, and fell to one knee.

'I said you ain't goin' nowhere. Git back in that chair.'

Shoot retched with pain – he had never been hit like that before. He backed away to his chair. 'You've no right to do that,' he gasped. 'This affair ain't nuthin' to do with me.' He put his hand inside his reefer jacket to grasp his side. It looked as if he was going for his gun.

The long-faced thug waved his revolver and covered him. 'Go on,' he jeered. 'Try me.'

Shoot winced and the man grinned yellow teeth. 'No? OK, stranger. Slowly now. Finger and thumb. Bring it out. Toss it over there.'

'These people need to be taught a lesson,' the captain said, as Shoot's six-gun was kicked away into a corner. 'It's all Ephraim's fault.'

'What shall we do with him, Cap?' Jem asked, eagerly.

'Make him kiss the gunner's daughter. Tie him over that barrel, Jem. Our friend Ephraim needs a little discipline.'

'No,' Ephraim screamed as he was hauled

up. 'You can't. You've no right.'

'Right. Right. Right. It's you who've no right, my friend. Tie him tight, Jem.'

The company moved uncomfortably in their chairs, but were silenced by the long-faced man's revolver.

'Twenty-five lashes. I'm going to be merciful. You would have had fifty if you'd been in my company. Insult an officer would you?' The captain was staggering on his feet and waving the bottle wildly. 'Use your belt, Jem. No, not the buckle-end. We don't want to kill him.'

Thwack! The belt whistled through the air and landed across the landlord's back as the burly Jem laid on with a will and a snarl of pleasure. Ephraim screamed and shuddered, and Shoot gritted his teeth as blood began to seep through the landlord's coarse shirt. 'Seven!' Slade shouted. 'Come on, Jem. You can do better than that. Put some weight into it, man.'

The men mentally counted each stroke as the captain's voice rang out. Ephraim had ceased screaming, but, his eyes closed, he shivered and gave a grimace of agony every time the belt came down.

'Fifteen. Good,' the captain said, spilling his whiskey. 'Sixteen. Good boy, Jem.'

The belt swished and Ephraim's legs twitched like a landed fish. Shoot gave a sigh of relief when the twenty-fifth stroke was reached.

'Go on, make it thirty for luck,' the captain said. 'While we're in the swing of it. I'm sure Ephraim won't object. He might be a little more civil to us in future.'

'It's a damned disgrace,' the Irishman protested.

'Ah, so somebody else wants some? I'll teach you.'

Captain Slade turned on his heel and lurched out of the saloon. It took some time for him to clamber on to his horse, trying to hold on to the bottle at the same time. When he did he charged the beast crashing into the bar, laughing and yelling, maniacally, as he scattered tables, chairs, glasses, and the sod-busters scrambled to escape. Shoot jumped out of the way with them, and made for the door as the captain whirled the horse around. The men ran in all directions as he chased them, and he laughed as he rode back and forth in the street trying to ride them down.

Shoot made for the safety of his room. He dived in and bolted his door and stood listening as the captain and his two bozos charged up and down the town. He heard them blamming away with their revolvers, smashing windows. He wondered how he would rescue his horse if they decided to burn the town down. But, eventually, things quietened. The captain and his boys must have returned to the saloon because he could hear a loud caterwauling coming from there – it couldn't be called singing.

He lay on his cot for a long while. He did not dare to fall asleep. In time, there was renewed laughter and shouting. He went out and stood in the shadows and saw the two men hoist the semi-conscious captain over his saddle. They climbed aboard their own broncs and led him at a jog out of town. Bear Paw, population 73, returned to the silent muddy township it usually was. Slowly, cautiously, doors opened, and men popped out of houses like weevils out of ship's biscuits. Shoot led the return to the bar to retrieve his revolver. Ephraim was still roped across the barrel. Shoot pulled his knife and cut him free. Ephraim groaned.

'You'd better put some salt in those lash wounds,' Shoot said to the curious crowd. 'I've witnessed worse floggings than that in the marine. I reckon he'll live.'

THREE

Shoot couldn't mistake Bannack City. The hills about it were a warren of mine-holes and unearthed spoil. Huts, cabins and tents were sprawled about higgledy-piggledy on the sides and bottoms of the gulches wherever men thought there was a prospect of gold. Scrawny women and snot-nosed kids hung around iron stoves that had been fixed up with chimneys in the open air, amid a litter of pots and pans. Maybe they intended to build a cabin around the chimney when they got rich?

The centre of the 'city' was similarly chaotic. Some hopeful had dug a tunnel under the main trail down through the town, which had collapsed, with the need for flatbed wagons, pedestrians, and horsemen to find a way around it through the deep mud. There were so many mules and buggies there was a parking problem and constant traffic jams. Men in dusty and crumpled suits watched the antics from the high sidewalks or wandered in and out of the numerous saloons.

Ramshackle log stores leaned one against each other down Bannack's main drag proclaiming 'Spring Beds', 'Wines, Liquors and Cigars', 'Brady's Billiard Hall', 'Gold Dust Bought', 'Mrs McGinty's Laundry, mending free of charge (Fortunes told)', 'Coal Oil Jim's Kerosene Store', or simply 'Ma Payne's', a shop with plucked ducks and chickens hanging outside, boxes of eggs, and churns of fresh milk. A proper little hive of industry, in other words.

There was a bank, dentist, drugstore, watchmender, and newspaper offices, *The Bannack Banner*, livery, and bath house. But, as well as the legitimate professions there were older and less salubrious ones. When Shoot explored the city's back lanes he had to step through lean-tos and shacks with crudely painted names like 'The Graveyard', 'Frozen In', 'Molly Muck's' or 'Try Again', where there was often a queue of miners at the door. They catered to the lusts and thirsts of men who shovelled and picked at the hillsides all day, and painted women openly flaunted their wares in doorways.

'Hi, mister,' a slim girl called, clutching at Shoot's sleeve. She couldn't have been more than fifteen. Her blouse was half-open at the front, and her unwashed flaxen hair hung down across her cheek. She had a sluttish, mischievous air. 'I'm only two dollars to you, sir.'

Shoot had to admit it: he was tempted. He swallowed hard as she dragged him into her dark hut and towards her filthy cot. 'No need to take off your boots,' she said, as he sat on the creaking bed. 'You ain't got all night.'

It was the dead tone of her voice that stopped him. It was clammy and cold, this transaction. No magic. No love. Something dirty and sad. 'No,' he cried, struggling up. 'I changed my mind.'

The slip of a girl smashed a tin bowl on his head.

'Come back, you bastard!' she swore foully and fluently as he dragged himself away and stumbled off into the night.

'Phew!' he said. 'That was close. Her attitude sure changed.'

When he had arrived in the late afternoon he had tethered his bronc with a nosebag of split-corn, and climbed around the gulches to inspect the claims. Some miners had dug shafts, others had a system of complicated rockers, there were those who used long sluice boxes, and lone, crazed-looking men who roamed about panning the ditches for paydirt. Many were downright unfriendly, growling at him to stay away. Another had erected a sign: 'Claim Notice – Jumpers will be Shot.'

Shoot wasn't sure how to begin. But he guessed he had to find himself a free spot and file his claim with the city registrar. This individual was a saloonkeeper, Fat Alex, who ran an establishment called the Montana Arcade and Dancing Palace. For Bannack it was high-class, with a long mahogany bar, polished floorboards, candelabras hanging from the ceiling, mirrors reflecting barrels and bottles, and a wide sweeping staircase that led to bedrooms above. The prices were sky-high, too.

A St Louis lager beer cost Shoot a dollar, when it would have been ten cents in more civilized parts. 'Like drinkin' gold-dust,' he muttered, more to himself, as he took a swallow, pressed in among the crush at the bar.

'Boom-town prices.' A stocky, barrel-chested fellow, his cheeks like burnished apples, and his hair a shaggy mat as thick as a mountain sheep's, grinned at him. 'Where ye thinkin' of puttin' that pick to work?'

'What pick?'

'The one ye tied to your bronc with the shovel and granite bucket. So happens I was watching ye over at the miners' emporium. Don't know much about this game, do ye?'

'Guess I'm a bit of a greenhorn. I'm twenty years old and I would have been here before now but I got held up by that damn war. Looks like most of the best sites have gone.'

'There's plenty more gold to be found. Ye're in luck. If ye're willing to work hard I'm looking for a partner for my claim. Ye strike me as a strong and reasonably honest young feller and there ain't so many of them around. How about it? I'm already bringing out good grade ore. We've every chance of a lucky strike.'

So, on the spur of the moment Shoot had a partner, a mine, and a new friend and was glad of it. 'Petroleum Jones is the handle,' the man said, sticking out his hefty paw. 'So-named on account of how I wasted my time boring out that new oil they found in Injin Terri'try. Only fit for burnin' in lamps. Gives off such a smell and there ain't no future in it.'

Petroleum had also worked down coal mines in Pennsylvania and seemed to know all the technical tricks of the trade. Shoot bought him a beer, but his senses pricked up when he saw the two thugs from Bear Paw push into the throng.

'Who are those two?' he asked.

'The one with the mangled haircut's Jem Stone, a misnomer if ever there was one. The tall one's Boon Helm. Two lousy sidewinders never done a day's honest work in their lives. You don't want to tangle with them.'

'I got a score to settle,' Shoot said. 'But I'll leave it for now.'

'Very wise, my friend. There's been a lot of stabbings and muggings. Several times the stage has been robbed some miles outa town. Rumour is they're part of the gang. But nobody's inclined to say so to their faces.'

The two men had joined a body of gamblers around a wide card table but, as he was about to sit down, Boon Helm noticed Shoot's regard. His dark, silvery eyes clashed with the youth's, and, as he licked his lips, his long, dark hairy jaws had the look of a hungry wolf's. One hand hovered over the butt of his holstered six-gun.

Shoot held his eyes for seconds and

turned away. Had the gunman recognized him? When he turned round again Boon had cast off his black hat and was riffling through a hand of cards.

'Who's the dude dealing?' A gent in a grey frock coat, boot-string tie, and waistcoat of watered silk was sitting with his back to the wall. He had a thick moustache and jutting goatee beard, his dark hair razored to curious pointed sideburns, not unhandsome, in a hard-cheeked way. 'Professional gambler?'

'Ye might say so. Henry Plummer. He's also been elected marshal of this fair city. There's killings every day over some trifle but he rarely bothers to investigate or arrest anyone. Too busy playing cards or chatting to the ladies.'

'Ladies?' Shoot had been unable to keep his eyes from a group of females in silks and satins herded behind a bar at the far end of the dance hall. 'Is that what they are?'

'Hurdy-gurdy gals.' They watched as the 'orchestra' struck up, roughly dressed miners dashed forward, and dragged the girls out into the hurly-burly of some dance or other. 'A dollar a dance. And for five dollars more you might git one to go upstairs. Top prices in this establishment. Ye wouldn't catch me paying that for a woman.

'That one. In the black dress. Would she, do you think?'

'She's a bit of a mystery,' Petroleum mused. 'Nobody knows where she comes from. I ain't never seen her go up them stairs. She don't look the type, does she?'

'No,' Shoot said, watching her.

'Only one way to find out. Go and ask.' Petroleum burst out laughing. 'Go on, enjoy ye'self, boy. But don't use all ye strength. I want ye down my mine in the morning. Ask around for my cabin when you're ready. Ye'll soon find me.'

She was a proud and graceful young woman, her brunette hair looped in coils, neatly parted and pinned to either side of her milky-white face. Her nose had a slightly Roman jut above a full, painted mouth. Her chin was strong, but her neck as slim as a swan's. She was the most soberly dressed girl in the house, in black silk and a plain white collar, whereas other women flaunted themselves in the loudest styles and lurid colours, their manners and laughter similarly blatant. Most of these harpies' curves were obviously assisted by padding at the bosom, hips and derrière.

The girl Shoot could not cease watching, however, although of a modest demeanour, was obviously all woman, her body trembling in the right places as she was swept around the dance floor in a quadrille. At that moment some *hombre* in greasy, fringed buckskins, his hair hanging to his shoulders frontier-style, a revolver and hunting knife on his belt, was making his spurs jingle as he swung her vigorously and kicked his boots. His partner gave him the regulation smile, but held her head back, somehow aloof – or maybe she was trying to avoid his buffalo aroma? Or his boots from tangling her ankles, or from stomping on her dainty high-heeled toes?

What was so delightful a young lady doing in this hurdy-gurdy house? Shoot wondered. She looked as if she would be more at ease in some society drawing-room. Surely she wasn't – and his stomach curdled at the thought – one of the upstairs girls?

'Promenade to the bar,' called the fiddler who led the orchestra, and in a flourish and swirl the dance was brought to a close with a stamping of heels. Shoot saw the girl extricate her fingers from those of the lean and hungry-looking frontiersman, who was pressing himself upon her. But, with a shake of her head, she left him and went to sit behind the wooden barrier at the far end of the hall with the other 'hurdies'.

He watched her settle down in her voluminous silk dress and fan herself, responding vaguely to an older woman in strident yellow ruffles who spoke to her. The girl shook her head some more, refusing several battered miners who made a rush for her. She was a very popular choice. But she obviously wanted a breather. Sure, she was a hurdy girl, all right, for whom the men paid a dollar a dance, and some much more. Her crimsoned lips and powdered face proclaimed that to be the case. But was she, at the same time, a whore?

The trouble was Shoot had never had time to learn to dance. But, for that matter, neither had most of these miners by the look of things. They mazurka'd around in a very rough and rumbustious style. 'At least I don't have bad breath, bow legs, cross-eyes, dandruff, spots, black teeth, or none at all, like most of these old geezers,' Shoot muttered to himself. 'And I don't stink like a polecat.'

He was perfumed, if anything, for, since getting into Bannack City, he had paid for a bath, shave and hair trim, and had bought himself a set of clean underwear and a fancy cross-over blue canvas shirt. He was trying to pluck up courage to approach this girl of his dreams. The musicians, who laid claim to the dubious title of orchestra – fiddles, harmonicas, a piano accordion and drums – struck up with a clash of cymbals and the dancers were taking their places for a polka.

Shoot stood in a corner of the crowded bar, sipped at a dollar 'tarantula juice' and, across the heads of the dancers, continued to study the girl, a deep longing in his guts. And all kinds of foolish romantic ideas about 'love' floated hazily in his mind's eye, as they often do among sensitive young men of his age. Others might have been more predatory and coarse.

What had he to offer her? Shoot Johannson by name: b. New York, father Swedish immigrant, and longshoreman; mother seamstress; fortune none, in fact, currently impecunious; former private soldier, merchant sailor; hair, blond; weight, ten stones; height, five feet eleven; eyes, blue; birth sign, Sagittarius; characteristics, honest (reasonably); strong sense of right and wrong but sometimes unable to act upon it; shy (very) with women; ambition, to go across there and speak to her...

It was no use shilly-shallying, or standing there getting pie-eyed. It was now or never. Similar promptings ringing in his head, he pushed his way around the gullumping mob of dancers and, his heart beating faster than it had when he was hanging for dear life to the top mizzen mast reefing sails above a maw of raging water, he was standing before her. 'May I have the next one?' he asked.

She glanced up at him through her long lashes, over her fan, as coolly as she did at all men, and Shoot's heart seemed to stop for long moments as he awaited her reply and noted that her eyes were an intense green, with darkly pronounced aureolas encircling the irises. Suddenly they seemed to sparkle as they connected with his, and she said, '1 presume, you've got a dollar?'

'Sure,' Shoot said, pressing the silver coin into her hand. 'Only I should warn you I ain't never done this before. I mean I'm none over-familiar with the steps.'

'Tell me another,' she smiled. 'Who is?'

'I guess it's pretty hard work? All these guys stamping on your toes?'

'It sure is. Just try and take it easy, will you? And follow me. There's fifty dances tonight and I want to survive at least thirty of them.'

'That's not bad money, thirty dollars a night.'

'Sometimes more,' she said mysteriously, and he wondered what she meant.

'Every night?'

'Most, except the Sabbath. Unlike most folk in this town I like to observe the Lord's Day.'

'I guess you need the rest. I mean you must be plumb wore out by–' He stumbled over the words which sounded somehow indelicate. 'What is your name?'

'Susan. But, let's get this straight, that's all I give away. You pay your dollar and have your dance. And don't ask, please, what a nice girl like me's doing in a place like this.'

'That's none of my business,' Shoot said, but already felt as if it was. 'I mean what you do's your affair.'

Susan gave a mocking downward grimace, and there was a wild pained look in her eyes as she tucked the dollar into her purse. 'I guess we're all here to make our pile the best way we can. And I'm not really fitted to be a miner.'

'You mine the miners, instead,' Shoot laughed.

'That's one way of putting it.'

The leather purse was suspended on a belt

in front of her like a sporran. 'I guess that gets pretty heavy by midnight,' he said.

'Like you said, that's none of your business. Come on' – that cold, distant look had come over her face again – 'they're taking their partners for a quadrille. Let's get this over.'

Heck, Shoot thought. Why's my mouth running away with me? I'm really ruining my chances. But it was pleasant to feel the girl's hand on his arm, directing him where to stand, to hear her say, 'Just do as the others do.'

The music struck up again and they were away. 'Step to your partners, forward and back, swing 'em round so you get the knack,' the caller called. This was no drawing-room quadrille, the men were swinging the girls almost off their feet, giving wild whoops of joy. The floorboards were bouncing fit to bust. And as he danced up to meet her Shoot felt like he was floating on a cloud. Their eyes clashed and for brief moments he had her body in his arms.

He finished out of breath and laughing. 'Wow!" he said. 'That was the best. The best dance I've ever had.'

'I thought you hadn't had one before.'

'That's the first and the best.' Her gloved palm was in his hand and, like the frontiersman before him, he did not want to relinquish it, but she shook her fingers free.

'Can I have another dollar's worth?'

Susan paused and looked at him with her green, misty eyes. 'Sure,' she said. 'Give me your money. Nothing's for nothing in this world. Only don't go getting any funny ideas about me.'

'What do you mean?' he asked, as he dug out another dollar.

'I mean I've seen that moony look on plenty of men's faces before. I'm not here to get involved with you or anybody.'

'Oh?' He registered this fact, despondently. It was something of a put-down. But he persevered. 'Couldn't I meet you when you're finished? Walk you back to wherever you live? I'd just like to talk.'

'Talk? Some talking most of you guys do!' She looked at him and again there was anguish in the wild whites of her eyes. 'Oh, maybe you can. You seem different. But only for a short while. It's true, I'll be exhausted.'

Their second dance was as exhilarating as the first. After that Shoot surrendered her to the pressing throng, and returned to his corner of the bar, slowly savouring a lager beer, warm inside, as he watched her being exercised.

FOUR

Petroleum Jones was a hard-rock miner. And his biceps were as hard as rocks to go with it. 'Dug it all out myself with pick, shovel, chisel and some discreet use of gunpowder,' he told Shoot proudly, as he stood in his tunnel, sweat trickling through the curly hairs of his beard and chest. 'See this dressed pine windlass. I made it myself. And I got some newfangled wire rope. Look at these pit props. Solid as the rock itself. Ye won't be havin' any trouble in this mine.'

'Where's the gold face?' Shoot asked, expecting to see a wall shining like Eldorado.

'Waal, ye'll have to wait awhile. We haven't got there yet. I'm a mite disappointed. I was pretty sure I was going to hit a main seam. What we'll do is sink a shaft down from here.'

Shoot was more than a mite disappointed, but he stripped off his shirt, spat on his palms, and set to shovelling away earth and rocks as Petroleum hammered with a big iron crowbar. For six days they worked in the glimmering light of little Humphrey Davy lamps as Petroleum's head gradually disappeared down from sight. But by Saturday they were none the richer.

Shoot bathed the dust from his weary body in a cold mountain stream, groaned at the ache in his bones, slicked back his flaxen hair and sat on a rock to shave with a cut-throat razor. He put on his clean set of long johns, frayed trousers, and new canvas shirt, tried to give a curl to the brim of his felt hat, and a polish to his dust-white boots, and cinched his thick leather belt tight. He had already lost weight. He could pull it in an extra notch. Must be all that bending and sweating, he thought.

He kept his percussion caps and lead bullets in different pouches on his belt, but decided he wouldn't be needing them. He wasn't going into battle! It might be advisable to reload his Colt and take it along though. It was a Navy which meant it had been made for the marines, but many had found their way into civilian use. It had an eight-inch barrel and a rubber-coated butt which made for surer grip. It was no easy matter loading. You had to know what you were doing. He raised the muzzle skywards, drew back the hammer to half-cock, which allowed the cylinder to turn in one direction freely. He snapped off a round of percussion caps, blew any oil or dirt from the nipples, and placed a charge of powder in, and a ball upon the mouth of the chamber. He pulled the lever, below the barrel, down. That wedged the ball tight into the chamber, and effected a hermetic seal.

'I see ye got one of them revolvers? It's an old one, ain't it?'

'Yes, old but good. Made in '47. I could ride through a river with this in my belt and it would still fire.'

'I've heard tell they're liable to blow up in a man's hand.'

'You gotta be careful. You gotta make sure all the balls fit the chambers snugly otherwise they might jar out and more than one chamber be discharged at once.'

'Ye expectin' trouble?'

Shoot decocked the pistol and stuffed it into his belt. 'Not really. I got a date for a dance with a beautiful hurdy-gurdy gal.'

'The one ye met last Saturday? How d'ye make out with her?'

'Oh' – Shoot shrugged, awkwardly – 'she let me walk her home, kiss her hand when we parted. You can't rush a young lady like her.'

'Let ye kiss her hand, did she? That was good of her. She strikes me as being somewhat high and mighty.'

'That's just her way. Maybe tonight I'll get to get a real smackeroo.' Shoot gave a wild yell. 'You comin'?'

'Sure. I'll take a stroll into town with ye. We've earned a beer or two. Won't need to be takin' me rifle if ye's all tooled up. Here, take a look at this.'

Petroleum put his curly-brimmed bowler to perch on the back of his curls and handed Shoot a large lump of glittering grey rock. 'Whadda ye think?'

Shoot pursed his lips. 'It don't look like gold to me.'

'Nor me, neither. I've just struck a seam of it. I'll take it into the assay office, see what he says.'

The two men hurried off down the hill headed for Bannack City.

'Well, look who's here,' Shoot cried, and he wasn't talking about the beautiful green-eyed Susan in her satin dress. He was talking about the man by her side, Captain Slade. 'We meet again.'

It wasn't just a spurt of jealousy, like acid in his insides, that made him speak out, it was the sight of the bullying Slade flaunting himself in tweed suit and gold watch chain like some respectable citizen. 'You ain't got your murderin' minders with you today, I see.'

'Do I know you, young man?' James Slade raised one eyebrow, quizzically, at Shoot's tone of mocking irony.

'Know me? You and your thugs relieved me of my revolver and made me watch you flog half to death some poor saloon-keeper. I should know you. Don't Bear Paw ring a bell?'

'C'mon,' Petroleum Jones muttered, gripping Shoot's arm. 'Ye don't wanna get involved with this gent. Let him by.'

They were standing on the wooden sidewalk outside the bank from which the captain and Susan had emerged. There was no way they could pass, unless Shoot made room, without stepping into the knee-deep gooey mud of the mainstreet.

Shoot was doubly incensed to see Susan on Slade's arm. 'I thought to find you at the hurdy-gurdy hall,' he said to her, insolently.

'Susan, you know this impudent fellow?' the captain asked.

'Hardly. He danced with me twice and seems to have the idea he owns me. He seems to be familiar with you?'

'Familiar? Yes, too familiar. I haven't the foggiest idea of who the devil he is. May I trouble you to step out of our way, sir?'

'You don't remember the saloon-keeper at Bear Paw? What was his name, Ephraim? Well, I do. I remember the mangled bloody mess you made of his back after you'd finished with him.'

'Ephraim?' The captain put one calfskin-gloved finger to stroke his moustache, as if there might be an unpleasant smell before him. 'Ah, yes. He had to be disciplined. He was very rude, you know. I've been to see him. We're the best of friends now.'

'Best of friends. Ha! I bet.' Shoot gave a scoffing laugh, and appealed to the girl. 'Is this, this drunken, cowardly bastard, the kind of man who appeals to you?'

Susan coloured up, haughtily. 'Get out of the way, you fool.'

Captain Slade raised his riding crop, threateningly. 'You're asking for a good thrashing. I'm warning you.'

'Try it.' Shoot pointed his index finger at Slade's nose. 'Go on. Try it. It's you will be getting the thrashing. Not me.'

'Hmm.' The captain stood, svelte and smiling, and put an arm around Susan's waist. He looked like a cat who was about to lap up the cream. 'I can see what's upsetting this boy. He's got a crush on you, my dear.'

'He's a fool,' Susan said, and her voice was shrill as she stared at Shoot. 'Go on, clear out. Or do you want to dig your own grave?'

Petroleum tugged Shoot to one side and they allowed the gentleman and his lady in her wasp-waisted grey overcoat, with its fur collar, to pass. 'What ye tryin' to do. Git yeself killed? The captain practically runs this city.'

He dragged Shoot by the elbow down a side street and into a bar called the Hangover Hole. As they entered Shoot turned and saw Slade and Susan standing watching them. A bitterness flooded his soul. 'They just make me mad,' he said. 'He does. She does.'

'Here.' Petroleum led him to the bar. He called for a bottle of rum and filled their tumblers to the brim. 'Get that down ye, boy. That's the wrong man to make an enemy of. Forget him. Forget her. She's not for you. She's a gold-digger but not the same sort as us.'

'Why does everybody keep calling me boy? I'm not a boy.' Shoot tossed back the musty rum. It gave him a jolt of fire. 'I'm a man.

And I need that woman.'

'Leave her be, Shoot. I'm warning you. What's all this about Bear Paw? Why didn't you settle it at the time?'

'His two bully-boys took my revolver. There wasn't much I could do. And, anyway, it wasn't my battle. The man was drunk, agreed. But when I saw him just now I had to give him my opinion, at least. And her.'

A wave of self-pity engulfed Shoot. He had been thinking all week about Susan as he laboured in the dusty, dark mine, dreaming of this night when he would be able to dance with her again, look into her eyes. He refilled his tumbler, tipped it to his mouth. 'Damn her,' he said. 'She's got me jumping like a cat on hot bricks.'

'Forget her. In my humble opinion she's no better than the doxies in doorways of a shanty town. Jest a higher class kinda hooer, thassall.'

Shoot turned to Petroleum and grabbed him by his shirt-front. 'No! Don't say that about her.'

'Calm down. Ye did right in Bear Paw. It ain't wise to interfere in these things. Go on, slug me, if it makes ye feel better.'

'Ah, go to hell.' Shoot pushed him aside,

took the bottle and went to sit at a table to one side of the sparsely furnished Hangover Hole. He took a deep drink and glowered at the rotund Petroleum, and his stupid, shaggy mongrel dog, Korky, who stood by the bar. There were only a couple of other customers, drab *hombres* who looked like they really had hangovers. And why not? Shoot thought. What else was there to do in this town but drink? By tomorrow he would have himself a big one. All he could think about was the cool beauty of Susan's pale face, the ludicrous little hat and veil perched on her satin-dark hair, the anger in her eyes when she spoke to him. Fool! Was that really what she thought of him?

He hardly noticed the two men who pushed through the batwing doors of the bar. 'Come ye here, Korky,' Petroleum called to his lop-eared adopted dog, who was sprawled on the floor scratching at his fleas. The two men were headed straight for him. And then he saw that the leading man was Jem Stone and he didn't step over the dog. He swung his heavy boot to kick it in the gut. Korky leaped away with a high-pitched squeal to cringe under a table.

'Hey, what ye doin'?' Petroleum's apple-red face went redder than ever. 'Don't ye kick my dog.'

'Keep your cur under control,' Jem Stone screamed, going equally red about the gills, his face contorted in ugliness. 'Dog shouldn' be here. I'll kill the damn cur if I want to.'

Shoot's heart had started pounding, for he saw that Boon Helm had followed Stone in, and gone to stand at the bar behind Petroleum. The lean gunman half-turned, jerked his black hat down over his brow, and his eyes gleamed maniacally as they glimmered over Shoot. He gave an evil grin. Shoot knew they had come to kill him.

'Nobody kicks me dog.' Petroleum was getting into a lather, taking off his jacket, laying it on the bar counter, placing his derby hat on top of it, rolling up his shirt sleeves, preparing for a fist fight. He looked as angry as a bull buffalo glowering out of his matt of curls. 'Ye step outside, we'll soon settle this.'

'Shut your face,' Jem shouted. 'Or I'll shut it for you.'

'Ye come outside,' Petroleum roared. 'We'll see about that. Or ain't ye man enough?'

'Leave it,' Shoot barked out, hoarsely, to his friend. 'Don't be the same fool as me.'

The rum had made his mind waver. He felt unsteady. He wasn't sure he could face Helm and Stone together. He didn't like the look of this at all. He put the rum aside and loosened his reefer jacket. He saw Helm give him a pitying smile as if he knew he was scared.

The stocky Petroleum was strutting towards the swing doors. 'Kick me dog would ye?'

'Sure I'll fight you, OK? You dumb bastard.' Jem pulled out his revolver and, with Petroleum's back half to him, there was the roar of an explosion. Petroleum had no chance. He was catapulted out through the doors.

Korky whimpered and raced out after him as Jem aimed him another kick. As the black powder smoke rolled, Jem turned his gun's deathly eye upon Shoot. 'Remember me?' he grinned.

The barkeep ducked down as Shoot slowly stood to face Jem. 'You've got the advantage of me,' Shoot said. 'You've got your gun in your hand.'

'Too bad. You think us boys play fair?'

As the revolver belched flame Shoot dived to roll along the floor, drawing his Colt Navy as he did so, cocking it, aiming it in one mechanical movement, and, as Jem's bullet smashed through a table leg, he fired. Stone sank to one knee, clutching at his chest which began to flower blood.

Shoot cocked and aimed again as Boon Helm snarled, drew his revolver, and blasted three bullets in Shoot's direction. The young Sharpshooter's lead made a hole in Boon's thigh, and he, too, toppled down, his thin face a grimace of pain.

'You want any more?' Shoot called, as he got to his knees, his Colt Navy pointed at Boon. 'If not, toss that gun away.

Boon held his regard as he clutched at his leg's bloody torn flesh with his free hand. After some seconds he decided not to chance it, and let his revolver fall. 'There'll be another time,' he growled.

'Get down on the floor. Face down, arms spread. Go on.' Shoot stood over Boon and kicked his gun away. He relieved him of a dagger from a sheath on his belt and went to look at Jem Stone. He was dead. His eyes had gone opaque and he stared blindly at the ceiling. The blood was spilling out of him making a scarlet pool on the floor.

The barkeep peeped over the counter; 'Jeez!' he said. 'Look what you done. The captain ain't gonna like this.'

Shoot strode out, the smoking Navy in his hand. A crowd came running. Petroleum was lying in the mud. His shirt was stained bloody at the shoulder.

'Are you OK?'

Petroleum's colour had drained from his face but he gave a pained grin. 'I'll survive.'

'I killed him.'

'Good.'

A shotgun was jabbed into Shoot's side. 'You're under arrest, son.' It was the Marshal of Bannack City.

Bannack City turned out in force for the trial. There must have been 500 miners crowded around the wagons in the barn where Shoot's case was to be heard, and spilling out of the doors. They had borne Petroleum Jones in on a stretcher, his shoulder bandaged up, to give evidence. He was a popular character and the miners stuck together when one of their own was attacked.

'I was shot in the back. My pardner killed the skunk. What else would you expect him to do?' Petroleum croaked, for he was still under the weather from the wound.

Doc Zabriskie confirmed that the bullet had indeed entered the shoulder from the back side angle, and, if not deflected by the bone, could have been fatal.

Boon Helm limped in on crutches to say Shoot started shooting first.

The barman, a nervous character in a celluloid collar, claimed he wasn't sure who started it. As Captain Slade glowered at him from the wagon he added that it might well have been Johannson.

The other witnesses in the saloon had conveniently 'gone prospecting' and couldn't be found.

Slade took the oath with a flourish, and in his cultured stentorian tones announced that the prisoner was a no-good who, prior to the slaying, had tried to pick a fight with himself and a young lady friend, on the grounds of some non-existent grudge. 'He threatened me in front of the lady and tried to force me to draw. I pushed him aside half-expecting to get a bullet in my own back. I do believe that he knew the men he shot were in my employ and he took his venom out on them.'

Judge Cyril Smith sat on the wagon beside him and didn't look too happy. 'There's a suggestion that one of them kicked Petroleum Jones' dog. That amounts to provocation.'

'Anybody kicked my dog I'd kill him, too,' one of the miners roared.

'Gentlemen,' Slade called, in his patronizing way. 'Let us be serious. The prisoner committed cold-blooded murder of the first degree. I demand that he be strung up. It is time we took a stand against these drifters and desperadoes who are drawn to Bannack City and make life a misery for honest folk. Don't be fooled by this young man's clean-cut appearance. I understand he is a deserter and fugitive from justice. If you err on the side of mercy I can assure you he will kill again.'

Shoot, who was chained hand and foot, was asked if he had anything to say. 'No,' he muttered. 'They shot my partner and drew their guns on me. So I killed one and wounded t'other. Shoulda killed him, too.'

After a lot of argy-bargy it was agreed to take a general vote. Those for hanging Shoot trooped through one of the barn doors, those against through the other. A good number, mostly those who thought it discreet to keep in with the captain, or who liked a good hanging, went through the 'for' door, some several times. It was a trifle chaotic. But the miners prevailed and Shoot was released amid whoops of triumph, with the proviso to be of good behaviour in future.

'You're lucky not to swing,' the nattily dressed Marshal Plummer told Shoot as he unchained him. 'Don't think this is the end of it.'

FIVE

'I hear you've been creating a name for yourself as a gunman.' The way Susan spoke sounded icily disapproving when Shoot bumped into her in the street the following Sunday. 'I guess you're proud of yourself at cheating the noose.

She was dressed, as before, in black silk and a clean white lace collar, and held a Bible in her hands as if just returning from church. Shoot's insides seemed to melt at the sight of her green eyes, which clashed with his, at the proud way she held her head, at the pale, purple-veined whiteness of her neck. She was wearing a crimson cape trimmed with otter fur and flecks of snow were sparkling on her glistening black hair, which was severely pulled back.

'It was self-defence,' he said, his heart thudding in his ribcage at this sudden apparition of her.

Susan coolly eyed him from boot to hat, her glance lingering on the long-barrelled weapon protruding from his coat. 'You're doing yourself no favours by antagonizing the captain,' she said. 'If I were you I would move on.'

'Does that mean you're concerned for my safety – or the captain's?'

'Guess.' Susan did not smile and went to pass by.

'I'd like to hope it might be the former,' Shoot said, and put out a hand to hold her arm.

Susan looked down at his hand with disapproval. 'Yes?'

'Would you?' he burst out. 'Would you have a drink with me?'

'It's the Sabbath.'

'That doesn't seem to bother anyone in this town. The saloons are open.'

'I'm sadly aware of that fact. What are you going to do? Get drunk and shoot somebody again?'

'Maybe, if you don't come with me.'

Susan gave a slight smile. 'If you were a gentleman like the captain I might invite you to my apartment for a cup of chocolate.'

'I'm as much a gentleman as Slade.'

'You really hate him, don't you?'

'I believe he sent those men to get me.'

'Gome along. Sundays do rather drag. But it can only be for a short while.'

She led the way along the sidewalk until she came to a sign that said, 'Lodging House. Good clean beds. Charges moderate'. She entered, took her key from the clerk, who peered over his spectacles at them, and climbed a creaking staircase to the third floor. 'I have two rooms to myself,' she said.

Shoot was surprised by the elegance of the first room, which had polished tables and chairs, a *chaise-longue*, carpets on the floors, and a log fire glowing merrily in the hearth. Susan drew the curtains and lit a lamp before going into the adjoining room which Shoot figured was her bedroom.

'Say, this is real nice,' he shouted.

'It's pleasant to have a few civilized comforts. We don't all have to be backwoodsmen.' She returned, divested of her cloak, and bent to poke some life into the fire. 'What would you like, tea or chocolate?'

She had a little spirit stove in the corner which she lit and put a kettle on. She spooned powdered chocolate from a canister and began to mix it with milk. 'It's nice to be able to have snacks. Makes it feel more like home. Sugar?'

'Please.'

'Take a chair. Relax.' She handed him the

steaming hot chocolate in a china cup and saucer. 'Tell me about yourself.'

He sipped at the sweet concoction and watched her settle herself in her rustling dress and underskirts like a dove into its nest. She perched on the *chaise-longue* and showed dainty black bootees and the hint of white-stockinged calves. 'They said at your trial you were a deserter.'

'You were there?'

'No, I read it avidly in the newspaper.'

'It's true. I enlisted with the Sharpshooters. Went through the first Bull Run. Just a plain infantryman. Marched here. Marched there. After my third taste of combat, when most of my friends had been killed or maimed, I began to think it was absurd. We were just like pawns on a checkerboard moved about by the generals of both sides. Ten thousand here. Take that hill. Whumpf! All wiped out. Nine thousand there. Whumpf! Another lot gone.'

'Didn't you see it as your patriotic duty to fight for the Union?'

'Huh! Patriotism? They can win the war without me. I decided I wanted to survive. So, I went home. Worked passage on a ship round the Horn. Up the Columbia to the Nez Perce reservation. Horseback from there. And here I am.'

'And you think you're going to make your fortune? Don't you know the odds against you doing that are a million to one? The same as the odds *on* you getting killed in the war.'

'So, you blame me for getting out, saving my skin?'

'Not really. Most of the people who come West are running away from something.'

'Right. Why isn't the captain with his regiment? Who is he to call me a deserter?'

'Not him again. You have certainly got a grudge against him. He is really an awfully nice gentleman.'

That stuck in Shoot's craw for moments, but he pressed on, angrily. 'What about you? What are you running away from?'

She glared at him, coldly. 'Let's say I'm one of those people in this world who doesn't take kindly to being ordered about by inferiors. Let's say I've come here because I can save more money in one month than I could in a year working as a shopgirl in Boston. My ambition is to get a nest egg, open my own business, so that it will be I who is doing the ordering.'

'Maybe we're two of a kind,' Shoot said. 'Because the same goes for me. I'd like to own my own business, maybe go into ranching.'

'Huh! You wouldn't catch me dead in some sod hut on the prairie. It's time for you to go.' Susan stood and took his cup, and Shoot felt a desperate pang that she was tossing him out into the cold street. He got to his feet and, as she turned from putting the cup aside, he grabbed her around the waist, pulled her into him and tried to kiss her. She jerked her face aside so his kiss slid from her lips across her cheek, and finished with Shoot's nose in her soft and scented hair.

'I want you,' he said, squeezing her to him, feeling the full softness of her breasts pressed against his chest. His sexual parts snapped to attention. 'I want you so much.'

'I'm aware of that. It's rather obvious,' she said with a faint smile, as she pressed him away. 'Please, Shoot! Don't!'

'I can't help it,' he cried, hanging on. 'I'm in love with you.'

'Let me go,' she cried, breaking away. 'I can't handle this. Why can't we be friends? Why do you have to be like all the rest?'

'I don't want to be just a friend. I can't be.' He looked meaningfully towards the open bedroom door. 'I'm desperate for you,

Susan. I don't want anybody else.'

'No!' Her voice was shrill, and her lips turned into a grimace. 'Who do you think you are? Why should I want you? A deserter! A miner! A murderer! Miners. You're ten a penny. You'll never find anything. You'll still be looking for the Holy Grail when you're sixty years old. Do you really imagine I'm going to give up my plan for you? I'm not going to be a hurdy-gurdy girl for ever. One of these days I'm going to be decent. I'll have a well-to-do husband, a fine home, lovely children, maid servants to run after me. I'll take my place in society. I'm not going to be some lousy miner's whore.'

Shocked by her words, her attitude, Shoot tried to hide his rampant parts with his coat and began to back out of the room.

'Yes, go,' she shouted. 'Don't come back here thinking you can be my lover, get me into my own bed for free. I thought you had some spark of gentility. You're just as filthy-minded as all the rest.'

Shoot skedaddled down the stairs like the devil was after him. Outside he leaned his back against the wooden wall and breathed in deeply. 'Whew! I certainly made a mess of my chances there.' But, as he groaned at his luck, he thought he could hear a faint sound of sobbing coming from one of the upper rooms. No, it wouldn't be her. She was hard as nails. He walked away to have himself a drink. He needed a bourbon. Ditch high.

Doc Zabriskie found Shoot sitting in The Hangover Hole morosely contemplating a half-empty bottle of bourbon.

'Mister Johannson?'

'Howdy-do, Doc. Call me Shoot. You slummin'?'

'No, I've been searching for you. This is not my favoured drinking hole. What you doing, visiting the scene of the crime?'

'You could say so.' Shoot pushed the bottle over. 'Join me.'

Doc Zabriskie poured himselt a tot. His grey fringe of hair fell over his brow. His lower face was encased in a neatly barbered white beard. His hazel eyes had a frank regard, and his face was wrinkled with laughter lines, a deep thinking furrow dividing his brows. His stout body was clothed in a hairy homespun suit of yellowy-brown 'butternut' colour. He had a gold pin in his stock and, like most men in these parts, wore heavy mud-daubed riding boots. 'You're a bit young to be ruining your liver with this rotgut, aincha? If you want my free professional advice you'll snap out of it.'

Shoot shrugged and poured himself another. 'Affairs of the heart, Doc.'

He looked so sad and serious Zabriskie had to laugh. 'You're not the first man to suffer. But it ain't no use killin' yourself over her.'

'What do you want with me, Doc?'

Zabriskie looked around as he lit a cheroot. The Hole as usual was more or less empty. 'I want words with you. Words of a life and death matter. So try and stay sober, will you?'

'Life and death?' Shoot looked up, his light blue eyes meeting the doctor's. 'Whadja mean?'

The doctor was carrying a Bible. Like Susan he must have been to chapel. 'Will you swear on the Good Book,' he said, huskily, pushing it towards Shoot. 'Will you swear that this conversation goes no further than us two?'

'I ain't got no faith. Seeing men slaughtered in the war kinda knocked it outa me.' Shoot pushed the Bible back. 'What's this all about? You can take my word for what it's worth I won't repeat this to nobody.'

Doc Zabriskie studied him and seemed to conclude he could trust him. 'I liked the way you gave evidence at the hearing. You appear to be an honest, upright young fellow. From what I've heard you can also take care of yourself. I'm looking for a man like you.'

'Me? Whadja want me for?'

The doctor sucked at his cheroot as he relit it, glancing around to make sure they were not overheard. 'You must be aware by now that this city is a sink of iniquity. It is full of the low, brutal, cruel, lazy, blasphemous, ignorant, insolent and depraved miscreants who infest the frontier. The rope is the only remedy.'

'The rope?'

'Yes? You take my meaning?'

'No. I can't say I do.'

Zabriskie took a deep breath again. 'My main practice is at Virginia City which, as you know, is some hundred miles further on from here. Shipments of gold have to pass through Bannack City on their way west to Salt Lake City, Utah. It's the only route. These shipments have not been getting through. The stage is continually being robbed. The honest and respectable citizens of Virginia City are getting sick and tired of it. Some of us have decided it is time to take the law into our own hands.'

'Shouldn't you offer your services to

Marshal Plummer?' Shoot asked. 'Raise a posse? Go, after these thieves?'

'Volunteering is out of fashion at the moment. There has been no draft. And the City Marshal has shown little inclination to track these road agents down. He is more interested in cards and whores than putting his life on the line.'

'You mean' – the penny dropped – 'you're organizing vigilantes? You want me to join?'

'You've got it. The committee had discussed you. We reckon you would be a good man. How about it, Shoot?'

Shoot stroked his jaw, and his Adam's apple bobbed as he swallowed. He looked worried. 'Aw, no. I've had enough of trouble. That marshal's tried to string me up already. I can't turn my back for fear of Boon Helm. I'm keeping my nose clean from now on. Count me out. I am surprised a respectable man like you's mixed up with a lynch mob, Doc.'

'We're not a lynch mob. We are all honest men who want to see a mountain society free of these pests. People are terrorized by these villains. Nobody dares give witness for fear of being killed. No jury will bring in a guilty verdict if the accused happens to be a friend of these badmen. They are openly intimidated. The exigencies of the times have rendered a little hanging necessary. Until, that is, we get a proper process of law in the Territory.'

'You're mighty persuasive,' Shoot said. 'Maybe you're not a mob. Maybe you *are* right. But I don't want to join. I got mining to do.'

'We are in the right,' Doc Zabriskie affirmed, putting his hand on the Bible. 'Every man in the committee votes on who to pursue and whether to exact banishment or the ultimate penalty. We don't go after a man lightly.'

'How many you got – you vigilantes?'

'About thirty at the moment. But we can't always all be on the qui vive. We have our businesses to run. We need younger men like you. You have no need to fear. We are all sworn to secrecy.'

'No. I'm sorry, Doc.' Shoot stood to take the bottle back to the bar and pay for what he owed. 'Don't worry. Your secret's safe with me. It's true, there's some dangerous people about. Somebody's got to call 'em. You're doing good work. I wish you luck.'

Zabriskie stared at his hands until Shoot had left the saloon. He stood, glowered at the barkeep, and went to find his horse.

SIX

'I'm sorry to tell you, son. It ain't worth nuthin'.' The assayer had a bald head and face the colour and shape of a parsnip and just as crinkled and dirt-engrained down to his scraggy neck. He held the glittering grey rock in his hand and blinked through his spectacles at Shoot. 'You better tell your partner he's plumb wasting his time and energy.

The assayer, known as 'Parsnip' Sessions, tossed the rock carelessly into a corner of his poky shop and turned to weigh a pouch of gold dust on his scales for a more fortunate customer.

'You think so?' Shoot had half-killed himself working for three long and hard weeks in the mine, for what? His few remaining dollars had all but gone. 'Surely it's got some worth? That glisten to it?'

'Fools' gold. How is that partner of yourn? Still alive?'

'He's recuperating well up at the cabin. Strong as a horse, eager to be back in harness. A bullet in the back ain't the finish of him.'

'I wouldn't be so sure.' Sessions gave a jerk of his head to Shoot, signalling with his eyes to wait until the other customer had gone. 'Now he's gone, I wanna warn you. Your lives ain't worth a brass nickel if you stay in Bannack City. You're a marked man. It's only a matter of time. Neither Boon Helm, nor the captain, care to be crossed.'

Shoot tapped his Colt. 'They know where to find me.'

'Don't be a fool, boy. They ain't likely to ask your permission for a fight.'

'Fool ... boy...!' Those words were beginning to irritate Shoot. 'Nobody's gonna run us outa town,' he said.

'You tell Petroleum what I said. He'll know I'm speaking horse sense. Look, I like you boys. I'll give you fifty dollars for that played-out hole of yourn. You won't get a better offer. I'm cutting my own throat, I know. Maybe I can find some sucker new in town to pass it on to.'

'I'll pass your message on.' Shoot stroked his chin and considered the offer. 'I could sure do with twenty-five dollars to make a new start. I'm kinda low on cash.'

'The new stampede's for Dry Creek

Canyon up back of Virginny City. They reckon they're picking up gold nuggets offen the ground. That's where you should head for. Make that pig-headed Petroleum Jones see sense.'

The assayer quickly looked away as another customer stepped in the store. 'So long,' he called. 'Don't shilly-shally over my offer. I might not be feeling so generous in a day or two.'

'So long,' Shoot muttered.

He didn't have much enthusiasm as he lit his lamp and went at a crouch along the tunnel. Like his hot calf love for Susan his ardour for this work had begun to cool. He gave a shiver, as he always did, when the daylight gave out and he was engulfed in cold darkness with only the glimmer of the Davy lamp. It was so eerily silent. The only sound was the drip of water through the rock, or a sudden heart-stopping creak as the earth somewhere moved. Men surely weren't meant to spend their lives down dark holes?

Shoot reached the new down-shaft and lowered a bucket on a wire rope. He clambered down after it with his pick. He wasn't sure what to do without Petroleum there. So he just began the hard mechanical labour of digging further and further down to see what he might find.

'Worth nuthin'.' He savagely slammed in the pick. 'Useless.' He studied the glistening blue-grey face and chiselled some more loose. 'Fool's gold.' He took off his shirt and wiped the sweat from his body. 'Maybe Petroleum ain't as knowledgeable as I thought.' Susan's face appeared before him and he swung the pick hard. 'Fool! Boy! Just a crazy miner. You'll still be doing this when you're sixty years old.' Her words of contempt returned to lash him.

Suddenly there was an almighty crash. Louder than thunder. An explosion at the entrance of the mine, booming along the tunnel, a hot blast of air, rocks raining down on him, billows of dust. Oh, my God! He froze, listening. Silence. He scrambled up, made his way through fallen rocks along the tunnel. And confirmed his worst fear. The tunnel was blocked by a mass of debris. He was trapped.

Petroleum Jones was lying on his bunk, his sturdy body bandaged tight by Doc Zabriskie, when he heard the sound of the explosion.

'What in tarnation's ... he ... doing?' Had Shoot taken it upon himself to accelerate his labours with gunpowder? 'Durned young fool.'

He struggled off his bunk and stepped to the door. As he did so he saw a man swing on to a horse and gallop away from their mine tunnel, which was belching a cloud of black dust. The rider had a bandanna covering his face, was dressed in dusty range clothes and tall hat, and was coming towards him ... he had a revolver in his fist and it was aimed at Jones. Petroleum rolled back as three bullets splintered into the door and walls of the cabin. Phew! That was close. He heard the clatter of hoofs as the rider went charging by. Another bullet smashed the window. Petroleum reached, frantically, for his loaded rifle and hauled himself up. He gasped with the effort as he got to the door and aimed at the rider's back.

'Damn!' he said. 'I missed.'

The rider would be out of distance by the time he had managed to reload the old 'long arm'.

'The dirty, filthy, murdering polecats,' he shouted as he used the rifle like a crutch to climb up to the mouth of the mine.

'Shoot!' he shouted. He stared at the solid mass of the cave-in, the discarded gun-powder barrel and fuse trail. *'Shoot!'* He knew it was no use.

Entombed. How long had he got? How long before his oxygen ran out? Or he died of thirst? It was an awful eerie sensation to be trapped in stone. To never see the blue sky again. Never see Susan's eyes ... no, he wasn't going to give up. He was lucky he wasn't injured. He still had his strength, his pickaxe. And he began hacking at the fallen rock.

In spite of the hole in his shoulder Petroleum Jones managed to get on to Shoot's piebald. He hung around her neck and cantered two miles into Bannack City to raise the alarm. The miners rallied in force. A hundred of them were soon marching back to the mine. They might be rough and ready, and ever eager to settle a dispute with a gun, but when it came to deliberate dirty tricks like this their ire was up. They worked in teams for two days and a night digging and shovelling and carting great rocks, bringing new timbers to make the tunnel safe, before they heard Shoot's voice and saw his dusty face through a crack in the rock.

'Jeez,' he said, as they helped him out. 'It sure is good to see you boys.'

When he was recuperated somewhat Shoot put his piebald into the shafts of Petroleum's flatbed wagon and laid his friend down inside. 'I ain't leaving you behind to be shot at,' he said, whistling to Korky. 'Looks to me like that wound of yourn's opening up and this place is getting plumb unhealthy. I'm heading for Virginia City.'

He urged the piebald through the mud of Bannack main street, pulling up outside the Montana Arcade and Dancing Palace. The sun was glimmering feebly as it sank from view behind the western Rockies. 'You'd better wrap yourself in that blanket. I ain't gonna be long,' Shoot said to his partner. 'You sure you didn't recognize anything about that fella who took the shots at you?'

'No. I've told you, Shoot. He had an old grey coat, batwing chaps, a red bandanna and hat. Dirty and dishevelled like any range hand. The only thing was his horse, a bay with a starlike blaze above its nose. An expensive horse.'

'I don't recall seeing any like that around.

Most of these are runty old plugs.'

'Don't ye go gettin' into trouble in there.'

Shoot hitched the piebald to the rail and gave him a grim smile. 'Would I?'

He pushed cautiously through the swing doors and strode towards the bar. Men fell silent when they saw the tall, blond-haired youth, the grim look on his face, and moved out of his way.

'Gimme a rum.'

Fat Alec passed him the bottle and watched him fill his glass. 'I hope you ain't thinking of causing any trouble,' he said.

Shoot tossed down the drink and felt the fire fill his throat. He gave a gasping smile. 'You worried about your fancy furnishings?'

With his back turned to them he could sense that Boon Helm was among the men playing poker at the big table in the corner, could sense that he was watching and ready for him. The orchestra was making all kind of scratchings and miaowings as it tuned up ready for the evening's entertainment. The swing doors opened and Susan came through. She paused as she saw him, her sea-green eyes widening with surprise. She walked across and Shoot's heart seemed to miss a beat.

'What are you hanging around here for?'

she said. 'Don't be such a fool. They'll kill you.'

Fool ... trouble ... don't do this ... don't do that ... he was getting tired of being told what to do. 'How much do I owe you for speaking to me?' he asked, not looking at her. 'A dollar?'

She jerked her head like a startled horse, her pale cheeks colouring. 'Go ... for my sake.'

'I'm looking for an explanation,' he said.

'It's your funeral.' She walked away to remove her coat, her bootees, to put on her high-heeled dancing slippers, to take her place with the hurdy-gurdy girls.

'Maybe it is. Maybe it ain't?' He turned and walked over to the men at the poker table. Boon Helm pushed a hand through his greasy, thinning hair, riffled through a pack of cards and began to deal.

'If you want to try to kill me again, Helm,' Shoot said. 'Here's your chance.' He eased back his reefer jacket and hooked his hand into his belt close to his gun butt.

'What's your quarrel?' Helm looked up and fixed his dark eyes on him. 'If you think I had anything to do with your mine you're wrong. So beat it. I'm busy.'

'You're a liar. A miserable no-good liar.

And a murderer. I'm holding you to account.'

'Who've I murdered, small fry?'

'Those two men out at Bear Paw for a start. You and Jem forced them into a fight. There's witnesses to that.'

'Now just hold on.' Henry Plummer had been sitting to one side. He stood up and stuck his thumbs in his cross-over silk waistcoat pockets. 'I've had enough of a punk like you causing trouble in this city. I happen to know Boon was sitting in a poker game here at this very spot the afternoon you stupidly used too much gunpowder at your mine. So don't come here making wild accusations.'

'I didn't use any gunpowder. You can get that idea out of your head. If he didn't do it he knows who did.'

'Me?' Boon gave his crooked grin. 'How the hell would I know? It's like the marshal says. You greenhorn miners ain't a clue what you're doing. Sooner you blow yourself to smithereens OK by me.'

The gang of ruffians sitting around the table cackled with mirth, grinning their blackened teeth at Shoot. He recognized Gad Moore, Clubfoot George, Montana Romaine, and Joe Pizanthia, the greaser, all 'no goods'. And there was a threat in the way they glared at him.

'Marshal *should* remember,' Gad sniggered. 'Boon won two hundred dollars from him.'

'Don't remind me,' Plummer winced. 'And for another thing, Johannson, I've investigated those deaths at Bear Paw. It was a fair fight. They drew on Boon and Jem. So unless you fancy being put back in irons you'll get out this saloon pronto. And outa this city. You ain't welcome here.'

'I'm gonna do just that, Marshal. Just as soon as I–' Shoot got hold of the big card table and hurled it upwards. Bottles crashed, cards spilled, men shouted and tumbled out of chairs. Shoot shoved the table hard up against Boon. He reached round with his left hand and dragged him out of there. His right fist smashed against the gaunt hairy jaw as he did so. And smashed again. He pushed his fingers up Boons nostrils and pushed his head back against the wall.

Boon Helm's boot came up and caught him between the legs. Shoot, nauseous with pain, saw him pulling his gun. He hung on to Boon's wrist, forcing it upwards, and a bullet crashed into the ceiling (taking a toe off a shopkeeper who was climbing into bed with a doxie upstairs). Shoot smacked Boon a vicious backhander across his cheek, wrested the revolver from his hand and hurled it clattering across the floor.

But Boon wasn't finished. He picked up a brass spittoon and clanged it across Shoot's brow, making him see stars, and followed up with a fist in his face, sending him crashing back over a table. Shoot was on one knee, shaking his head, when Susan screamed, 'Watch out!' Instinctively Shoot ducked as Boon's hunting knife whistled past his ear and hammered into the wall.

He dived back at Boon, running the tall, wiry gunman back against the bar. The miners, gamblers and girls cheered and shouted as the two men grappled with each other, swaying back and forth, breaking apart and swapping punches. Shoot feinted with his right and put in a piledriver of a left, knocking Boon flailing back to the bar. He held himself up on it, reached for a bottle, smashed it, and, his eyes venomous, struck out at Shoot.

The young New Yorker dodged three such sallies, managed to grip Boon's wrist and back-jabbed his elbow into his throat. Helm dropped the bottle and went down croaking with pain. Shoot gave him a kick in his solar plexus to help him on his way. Boon stayed down, choking, holding his throat.

Shoot sucked on his knuckles and tried to catch his breath. He had his revolver in his belt but he left it there.

'I owed you that,' he gritted out as Boon groaned. 'For old Ephraim. For everybody. Shooting's too good for you, you weasel. One of these days I'm gonna watch you hang.'

Shoot's speech was cut short as Marshal Plummer's revolver butt clubbed him across the back of the ear and he went down on one knee, his head spinning. 'Throw him outa here,' Plummer yelled.

Gad Moore and Joe Pizanthia laid some kicks into Shoot and he rolled and crawled half-conscious between them, until they hoisted him up, dragged him out to the sidewalk, and hurled him face down into the sucking mud.

As they did so Boon Helm was helped to his feet, screaming, 'Kill him!'

The city marshal strode out and stood among the men jeering at Shoot from the sidewalk as he tried to pick himself up. He raised his revolver, cocked it and aimed. 'You saw him,' he said. 'Resisting arrest.'

'I wouldn't do that if I were ye, Plummer.' Petroleum's voice rapped out from the wagon. He was lying there, his old longarm at his shoulder, aimed unwaveringly. 'Nor any of ye others. The marshal gits it first, if it's the last thing I do. Put that gun back in your belt, Plummer. Git up here with ye, Shoot.'

Shoot stumbled about, trying to stay on his feet, trying to wipe the mud from his hair and eyes, trying to get back on the wagon. When he was on the box he pointed a finger at the marshal and shouted, 'If you ain't prepared to lay down some law in this town, Plummer, I'm gonna find who is.'

He saw Susan looking over the batwing doors among the crowd. At first she had appeared anxious, but now she gave a deprecatory smile at his ignominous exit. 'The boy never seems to know when he's beaten,' she said.

'I ain't beaten,' Shoot muttered. 'C'mon, giddap.' He flicked the reins. 'Let's git out of this shitty city.'

Petroleum lay in the wagon, his long rifle pulled into his uninjured shoulder, finger on the trigger, aimed at Plummer. He kept it like that as they trundled out to the city limits.

'I had 'em, covered,' he piped up. 'That's why they didn't shoot ye, Shoot.'

'Yeah, thanks partner.' Shoot wiped mud from his ear that was still stinging from the marshal's blow. 'I guess they'll try again when there ain't nobody around.'

'Moon's fit to rise. If you take my advice ye'll put some miles 'tween us and this city afore midnight.'

Two hours must have passed and they were rattling up a rocky incline, the piebald doing her best but slowed by the climb, when they heard the sound of horsemen behind. The big full moon had indeed risen and illumined the harsh terrain a striated silver and black, and, looking back, Petroleum called out, 'They're gaining on us. There's a good dozen of 'em. What do ye reckon they want?'

Shoot licked his lips and yelled at the piebald to go faster, but the flatbed wagon was too heavy for her. 'I've a purty good idea,' he shouted, and hauled the horse in, jamming the wagon against a wall of rock. 'Wish I still had my Sharps. One revolver ain't gonna be much use against this murderous mob.'

'Its been good knowin' ye, boy. Maybe we'll meet in another life.'

'I ain't gone yet,' Shoot muttered, and dropped down to lie behind a back wheel, cocking his revolver in readiness.

'Get back, Korky.' Petroleum rolled over and poked his one-shot Kentucky through the tailboard. 'Let me get a bead on those dog-kickers. At least I'll have time to take one of them with me.'

The gang of horsemen was almost upon them and had started loosing a volley of shots. Lead whanged and whined about the wagon chopping sharp splinters from the wood. The Kentucky boomed and one of the leading riders pitched to the ground. 'One for the pot!' Petroleum cried, and reached for his ramrod to begin the laborious process of reloading.

'I wish I knew which one was Boon Helm,' Shoot said, as he squeezed his revolver trigger and saw the men rein in and mill round. In the dark, with bandannas over their faces and in range clothes, the horsemen looked much alike. Their weapons spurted flame as they made Shoot duck his head down and he heard their howls and curses as one called, 'Move in, boys.'

Some had dismounted and were firing from cover, others riding their mounts up to surround them. Shoot had the satisfaction of seeing two more drop from their saddles, and another squealed like a pig and shook his arm as if he'd been hit in the wrist. Shoot chose his shots slowly, hoping to keep them off until Petroleum had time to reload. But the gunmen were darting forward through the rocks like sneaking coyotes, closing in for the kill. Once his six were spent ... it was only a matter of time. Like Petroleum said, they couldn't fight them all off.

Dust spurted into his eyes as a bullet nearly took off his ear, ricocheting off the rocks. It sure was difficult to aim under such a barrage. He fired twice to no avail. He squeezed again and there was an empty click. 'Hot damn!' Shoot drew his knife and crawled back behind the wagon. Petroleum was still trying to put powder in his flintlock. This was the end for sure.

Suddenly, however, other shots were being fired from up the trail behind them. What was happening? There was a clatter of iron-shod hoofs and a wild whooping as a posse of men came charging down towards the attackers. Shoot saw several of the Bannack men take lead and fall. Surprised, others were leaping on to their broncs and turning tail. The skirmish was short, if violent. The badmen weren't prepared for this. Carbines and revolvers blazed as they backed away, and set off full gallop down the trail, back towards Bannack City, chased by the rescuers, whoever they might be.

They, too, were dressed in dark, dowdy range clothes, most with bandannas round their faces, and some with full hood masks, their slits of eyes giving them a spine-chilling appearance in the moonlight.

One of them turned and rode up to the wagon. 'You men OK?' His mask muffled his words, and a duster riding coat enclosed his stocky body.

'Thanks to you we are – just!' Shoot called. 'Is that you, Doc?' For he thought he recognized his voice.

'None of us here have names,' the rider said.

One of the men had lassoed the gunman who had been shot through the wrist, and was hauling him towards them. His bandanna had fallen from his face and he was moaning, piteously, holding his bloody hand.

'It's Clubfoot George,' Petroleum shouted. 'He's one of Boon Helm's whippets.'

'Is that so?' The stocky man in the mask looked down at him. 'Who was leading you, George?'

'I don't know, I swear. I was just riding along for the safe company when these two opened up at us as we came up the pass. Jesus! My wrist! Do something for me, please.'

'We'll do something for you. I asked who you were with. I reckon he needs some memory powder, boys.'

The men had returned from chasing off the attackers. They were all masked, and, in the moonlight, they had a frightening appearance as they gathered around Clubfoot.

'Why not run the wagon wheel over that injured wrist of his,' one said. 'He won't go round shootin' at people again.'

'No!' Clubfoot howled. 'OK, I'll tell you, boys, even though they'll kill me for it. It was Boon and the marshal sent us out.'

'The marshal?'

'Yeah. He reckoned these two were wanted for somethun'.'

'So you reckon you're a kinda posse?'

'Yuh, that's it.' Clubfoot George was quick to agree. 'A posse.'

The stocky man, who appeared to be the leader, asked, huskily, 'How many of us believe that? Those who do step to the far side of the trail.'

None of the men moved. Their eyes stared stonily at Clubfoot George. He was a renowned villain, bully and murderer. 'What's it to be, boys? A hempen necktie? For the attempted murder of these two men? Those who say, "Aye" step to the other side of the trail.'

Almost as one the men moved to line up along that side of the trail, and the man with his lasso around George began arranging it around his neck. Clubfoot George began to stutter and quail. 'Have a heart, boys. You can't mean this, can you? I told you what you wanted to know. Please...'

The leader sat his horse and pointed to a stunted pine that jutted from the rocks. It had one sturdy branch reaching out across the trail as if made for the rope. The man on the horse took the rope end and tossed it over the branch. He caught it and tied it to his saddle horn. 'You got anything to say ... any last request?'

Shoot watched the eerie scene with a sense of horror as Clubfoot was placed under the tree.

'These sure are tight papers, boys,' Clubfoot stuttered. 'I thought you and me was pals.'

And he was lurched up into the air as the

leader spurred his horse forward. He was kicking and swinging and, pathetically, reaching for his empty holster with his good hand as if to bring out, cock and fire a revolver at them. Some of the vigilantes laughed, it looked so ludicrous. It was some moments before Clubfoot's kickings and twitchings ceased. His suffering was over – or about to begin?

'Leave him there. Let folks mark this as a hanging tree. And those other dead. Pile them up beneath. Let people know we've passed.'

Shoot was standing beside the man who had put the rope around Clubfoot's neck. 'Didn't you feel anything doing that?'

'Sure, I felt for his ear.'

'You, Mister Johannson, had better head on your way to Virginia City. We may have more hanging to do tonight. I told you before,' the masked man said, 'the rope's the only remedy.'

SEVEN

Virginia City, Montana Territory – not to be confused with the larger gold-boom city of the same name in Nevada Territory – was well laid out with some substantial stone and wooden houses, bank, stores, church, and hotel, the miners' shanty town being confined further down the mountain trail. It was more orderly than Bannack City. That is to say, instead of muggings, knifings, and shootings every day of the week, they happened at Virginia City usually only on Saturday nights.

'This town used to be as bad as Bannack,' the gent who ran the assayer's office told Shoot. 'We've got the vigilante committee to thank that decent folk can walk the streets unmolested at night.'

Shoot had taken in a couple of chunks of the blue-grey rock. 'I kinda thought we oughta have a second opinion,' he said.

'You leave that with me, young fella,' the assayer told him. 'I'll give it a look over. Cain't say it looks too promising. Where you headed now?'

'Up to Dry Creek Canyon.'

'You're wasting your time. Bottom's already dropped out of that stampede. You'll be lucky to make more than five dollars a day.'

'That's OK by me. That'll be five dollars more than I've got in my pocket now.'

Petroleum wasn't too flush, either. He'd sunk most of what he had into his Bannack mine. They had barely enough for some groceries, a bag of corn and a block of salt for the horse. Jones looked somewhat grouty, or peevish, as Shoot helped him back on to the wagon.

'You know, there is one way of getting rid of that old mine,' he remarked, as they trundled out of town past a gang of Chinese, in their pigtails and baggy blue clothes, who had just arrived on the stage. 'Sell it to these Chinks.'

'How come? They're not that stupid.'

'What ye do is ye fill a shotgun with a poke or two of gold dust and splatter it on the wall of your mine. Then ye show those Chinks the seam. They'll think it's pure gold. I reckon they got plenty dollars tucked under those smocks of theirs.'

'Ain't that kinda dishonest?'

'Pah. It's a tried and trusted way of getting rid of a useless mine. Ye'd be surprised how many greenhorns been fooled that way.'

'Well, we don't even have one poke of dust,' Shoot said. 'I'm beginning to think I've come to the wrong territory. Hear tell they're minting pure ten-dollar gold drops in Denver, Colorado. And on Idaho's Salmon River they say the only shortage is cans to store the gold dust in.'

'And how ye gonna git to Idaho?' Petroleum asked. 'This nag's on her last legs.'

Their spirits did not rise when they reached the bedraggled tents at Dry Creek. Many of the prospectors were packing their mules and moving on. The placer dust was running out. Most were only averaging ten cents' worth of dust per pan.

'We'll give it a try,' Petroleum said and, his wound much improved, he began sniffing round for a suitable site. The melting snows had sent a stream of water down the creek, and they spent their days panning for gold. Petroleum showed Shoot how to shovel sand into the pan, submerge it, and spin it slowly to wash the sand out over its rim.

'Hey!' Shoot cried, his heart leaping, as he saw a comet tail of gold specks on the bottom of the pan. 'Look at that!' With a knife he scraped up his gleanings into an old tin can and set to again. But it was hard work, and after squatting all day in a cold mountain stream, he was lucky to get five dollars worth of dust.

Five dollars was five dollars, though. They persevered and transferred their dust to leather pouches and, after three weeks of labour, Petroleum announced he was returning to town. Shoot had also been excited by finding two small button-sized nuggets, soft enough to bite into, of pure gold. 'There must be a crock of it around,' he said.

'Sure, at the end of the rainbow. We're wasting our time. I reckon ye were right. We should head for Colorado. They say a fella called Gregory's just been paid twenty-two thousand dollars for his mine. That's my kinda scene.'

So they returned to Virginia City. When Shoot weighed in his dust and small nuggets he found himself richer by $150. It wasn't the big time, but it helped.

Shoot bought himself a second-hand carbine and another ten-dollar revolver. 'I've come to the conclusion a man needs to be well armed on the trail hereabouts,' he told Petroleum, as they tucked into pig's head stew and cabbage in the Idaho restaurant.

It was then he remembered the rocks he had left with the assayer, so, after coffee, whiskey and a cheroot, he strolled around to his shop out of curiosity.

'Good heavens! I been wondering where you boys had gotten to.' The assayer, who had a reputation for straight dealing, put the rock on his counter. 'I could hardly believe the results of my tests. So I repeated 'em with the utmost care. This here's galena. There's a mixture of silver and gold in that rock. I estimate it at two thousand dollars in silver and five hundred and seventy dollars in gold to the ton.'

'You mean that's what this rock's worth?'

'No, I mean you dig out a ton of this stuff and that's what it will be worth. How many tons you reckon you got in that seam?'

'I don't know,' Shoot said, somewhat taken aback. 'Quite a few, I think.'

'Where is this mine, son? You'd better be gettin' back there pronto 'fore some sonuva-bitch jumps your claim. I ain't said nuthin' to nobody, but these things have a habit of getting out.'

'Jeez!' Shoot gasped, as he backed away to the door. 'I better go find my partner. And thanks!'

Shoot's excitement, however, was dampened as he walked down Jackson Street past John S. Rockfellow's general merchandise store – 'All kinds of country produce, staple and fancy groceries' – for he saw Captain James Slade, in his dark Union greatcoat, talking to the Mayor, Joe Castner.

They were standing outside Wells' and Fargo's stage office and a coach, pulled by a team of six, was about ready to move out. The mayor signalled to a clerk standing in the doorway of the bank across the way and two guards came out hauling a strongbox. They hoisted it up to the stage driver, Cyrus Skinner, who thrust it beneath his seat. One of the guards, with his shot-gun, jumped up beside him. The other climbed inside. They were taking no chances. Skinner gathered his reins, cracked his whip, and the coach went lumbering away out on the Bannack City trail.

Captain Slade watched them go, slapped the mayor on the shoulder, and strode back into the stage office. Castner walked away towards his lawyer's office situated over the Idaho Restaurant (which he also owned).

'Excuse me, Mister Mayor,' Shoot said, falling into step with him. 'Can you tell me just what Captain Slade's got to do with the stage line?'

'Why, he's the agent for Wells and Fargo in Montana. He also handles mule transportation of heavy equipment from Fort Benton to this city and all the other mining camps, Helena, Deer Lodge City, Diamond City and Bannack. The captain's a big wheel in this Territory.'

'I thought he was a rancher.'

'No, that's just a sideline. He's got fingers in many a pie. Why, what's your interest, boy?'

'Nothing; just curious. Hear tell you've had a spate of robberies of the stage.'

'That's true. We've doubled security, as maybe you noticed.' The mayor, a skinny character, in dark frock coat and Lincoln hat, paused to light a cheroot and eyed Shoot, astutely. 'Ain't you the young fellow who had a run-in with Captain Slade a while back?'

'Aw, that's best forgotten,' Shoot said. 'I'm just wondering if there would be a reward for the apprehension of any of these road agents.'

'Well, I guess there might be.'

'And I'd be right in surmising that when there's a big shipment of gold from the camps, Captain Slade, the bank, and you would be the only ones who know about it?'

'That's true, apart from the driver and the guards, of course. What you trying to say, son? You still harbouring a grudge against the captain? You can drop any of those ideas. He's a pillar of society in this Territory.'

'Apart from when he's drunk?'

'Ach, agreed; he goes on a spat. But that's only now and again. It don't interfere with him doing his job. You needn't think it does. There's talk of him standing as senator. He's a very popular man.'

'Yeah,' Shoot muttered. 'With some.'

He rustled up Petroleum, gave him the good news, and they spent most of their Dry Gulch dust on a big bay carthorse to help the piebald in the shafts. They made it back to Bannack in two hard-hauling days.

'That seam could run for a mile and hold a million tons. At two thousand five hundred a ton we'd be billionaires, boy. Even if we could only dig out a thousand tons we'd be on easy street.' Petroleum was assessing their from-rags-to-riches future non-stop as they drove. 'Or maybe we should sell out to some big company that's got the heavy equipment and organization behind 'em.

Don't you ask for less than fifty thousand for your share Shoot.'

'I sure could buy myself a nice little spread with that.' Shoot whipped the horses on and smiled at his partner's excitement. 'On the other hand, don't you think we oughta count our chickens when they're hatched?'

'Aw, how can ye be so mealy-mouthed? I'm gonna call it The Johannson-Jones Galena Mining Company Inc. Or maybe Jones-Johannson. Which d'ye think's got the best ring? If it weren't for ye gettin' a second opinion we could have lost out on this...'

His words trickled out as they passed through Bannack and rattled up the mountainside to their mine. A barricade of felled trees had been placed across the trail with a notice: *Plummer and Helm Silver and Gold Workings – Danger of Explosions – Uninvited Visitors Keep Out – Guarded Premises.*

'What 'n tarnation...?'

For moments Petroleum was dumbstruck. And then he jumped down and began clearing the trail. 'We'll see about this.'

A bullet whistled and whined from a sentry post taking Petroleum's derby hat off. 'Keep away from the barrier!' A voice was hailing them through a megaphone.

'Put your weapons aside and your hands up. We will come down to talk.'

Shoot and Petroleum looked about them. Wire rope had been strung to mark off the environs of their mine. Several wagons with mining equipment were parked outside their cabin. And the sun glinted on rifle barrels of guards nestled in strategically placed boulder-built gun-emplacements about the hillside. The mine was as impregnable as an army fort.

Slowly they raised their weapons and laid them aside and put up their hands as a group of horsemen approached. Shoot swallowed his gall as his eyes met those of Boon Helm, who gave a crooked grin, pulled in his mount on the far side of the barrier and leaned on his saddle horn. 'Well, boys,' he drawled, as he pulled some tobacco-makings from his leather waistcoat, 'what would be your business here?'

'This here's our mine, ye lousy claim-jumper,' Petroleum yelled. 'Get this barricade cleared. An' ye all get outa here, you hear?'

Helm was sided by the Mexican, Joe Pizanthia, whose gold teeth gleamed as he laughed and he fingered a shot-gun held across his chest, and by the dark-jowled

Montana Romaine, as iron-nerved a man as ever levelled a six-gun. They were backed by half-a-dozen sour-faced *hombres* in tall hats and leather chaps, one of whom drawled, 'Who's gonna make us, fatso?'

'No use you two makin' trouble,' Helm warned. 'This mine's been left unattended for three weeks and by miners' law that means it's ours for the taking. And we've taken it. There ain't no way you gonna git it back.'

'You warned to get out of this city.' Pizanthia's voice had the threat of a hissing rattlesnake as he thumbed back the hammers of his sawn-off. 'Why you not take good advice?'

'Yeah.' Montana snarled at Korky who had begun to bark a challenge at them. 'That damn mongrel of yourn sure gittin' on my nerves.'

'Leave 'em, boys,' Boon shouted, jerking his horse away. 'They ain't got a leg to stand on. Remember, this is private property, legally filed. If they try to get past that barricade, shoot to kill.'

'C'mon,' Shoot said, jumping down to turn the wagon. 'Let's get outa here. There ain't nuthin' we can do ... for now.'

Petroleum's ire was up. He stormed into Bannack City protesting to all and sundry. He marched into the Montana Dancing Palace with six miners behind him. 'I ain't serving you,' Fat Alec said. 'You owe me for the damage last time.'

Shoot grabbed him by his bald skull and smashed it down on his own bar counter. Alec unfortunately hit a glass and came up bleeding from the brow. 'You fiddling bastards owe us,' Shoot said. 'You're all in this.'

Marshal Plummer stuck a gun in his back. 'You again, eh? It's the big jump for you this time.'

'You're in it, too,' Petroleum cried. 'That's my mine you stole.'

'Talk sense, Jones. You miners know by your own law if a mine's left unworked that long it's open to a new claim. And we've made one with Fat Alec here.'

'Yeah, but I wouldn't have left it if I hadn't been lied to by that pal of yourn, old Parsnip Sessions,' Petroleum protested.

'More fool you for believin' him,' Fat Alec whined, wiping the blood from his face. 'Arrest 'em, Marshal.'

'That's my mine, boys,' Petroleum persisted. 'They got it from me by false pretences. Ye all know that.'

The miners shook their bearded heads and looked dubious. 'It's true what the marshal says. It's miners' law.'

'I'm giving you two one last chance. I'm not putting you in chains for this assault,' Henry Plummer said. 'I'm letting you go with a caution. And that is, get out and keep going this time.'

They left the saloon and surveyed the goings and comings on the muddy main street. 'What now?' Shoot asked.

'Come on. I ain't finished.' Petroleum led him to the office of Cyril Smith, a legal eagle, who had never done any good back east but found the violent west ripe for plucking. He handled numerous tangles over mining rights and, being the only man around Bannack with law knowledge, had been appointed judge. His twenty-stone bulk made his office chair groan. But all he gave them was an oily smile and a lot of legal jargon.

'You can sue, gentlemen,' he said. 'But what it boils down to is you ain't got a snowball in hell's chance. By the way my bill for consultation is ten dollars. Kindly pay my clerk as you go out.'

Petroleum was so brow-beaten by now he

coughed up without a murmur. 'Oh, Jesus,' he groaned. 'I was planning to buy me a yacht and take a world cruise.'

'And I was thinking I could be married,' Shoot said, glumly. 'If I had half a million in the bank Susan might not look so down her nose at me.'

Later, Doc Zabriskie, who was in the city on business, stood them a rum in The Hangover Hole.

'I guess we gotta thank you for saving our lives,' Shoot said. 'The way you and your men turned up outa the blue the other night.'

Zabriskie frowned. 'I don't know what the hell you're talking about.'

'But, wasn't it you–?' Petroleum began until Shoot kicked him under the table.

'I'm sorry, Doc,' Shoot said, noting the waggling ears of the barkeep. 'I got a real bad chest complaint. Could I have a private consultation sometime?'

'Come to my surgery at seven tonight,' Zabriskie snapped, and strolled out.

'What's the trouble,' he asked, when Shoot faced him across his desk.

'I want to join. I'm sick to death of the log-rolling and back-stabbing goes on in this Territory.'

'We don't welcome any man to our committee who's simply there to avenge a personal grudge.'

'OK, we've got a grievance. But it's not just that, Doc. I reckon we can say goodbye to the mine. It's some justice I want. Why should these thugs run roughshod over decent people? It's not just my case. I see it everywhere. For instance, that Captain James Slade, he shouldn't be allowed–'

'That couldn't be another grudge, could it, Shoot? Sure the captain goes on a drunk and maybe shoots up a store, but he pays in cash for his folly afterwards. He's got a lot of support in this Territory.'

'Hmm? Couldn't be, could it, Doc, that you vigilantes are prepared to string up some no-account no-good, but when it comes to a man with money, somebody of social standing, that's a different story?'

'I'll tell you something I didn't ought to, Shoot. Captain Slade has ridden with the vigilante committee and given good service. He's as much concerned at getting some law and order in this Territory as any man.'

'He–?' Shoot's mouth opened with surprise. 'He's one of you?'

'We don't normally mention committee members by name. Silence and secrecy is necessary to fight the desperadoes who terrorize the country. They have their own secret organization, their spies everywhere. That's why I didn't like what you said in the saloon.'

'Yes, I'm sorry. I realized as soon as I opened my mouth. But, Slade – you're right, I hate the man – I just couldn't ride with you if he's along. He's probably there purely for the pleasure of seeing men hang.'

The doctor gave a pained grimace. 'Maybe we all get some pleasure from seeing a bad man swing.'

'No. He's a sadist. He goes along for the fun of it. I wouldn't trust him if I were you, Doc.'

'Well, you ever get any real proof against him, you let me know.'

'Maybe I'll just do that.'

EIGHT

Henry Plummer stretched and wiped the sweat from his naked limbs with the blanket. 'That was real good, honey.' He ran a hand over the woman's warm, voluptuous breasts. Beautiful breasts, nipples like organ stops when she was aroused. And aroused she was all right, hot and breathing hard.

'Is that all I get? Aren't you going to do it again?' She reached a rough hand down to hold on to him.

'Sure, jest let me wet my throat. Don't Jan keep no whiskey in this dump?'

'No. He say it no good for man.' She was a big-boned Norwegian woman, her hands and face reddened and roughened by weather and work, her body heavy from child-bearing. 'He don' know what he miss, eh?'

'Pass me that pitcher of water, then, Helga. As soon as I start pulling riches out my new mine it's gonna be champagne every day for you and me.'

'You will take me, won't you, Marshal?'

She looked at him, anxiously. 'You won't leave me here?'

'Sure I will.' He slapped her rump as she leaned over to reach for the pitcher. 'San Francisco here we come. We'll take a mansion on Nob Hill. You'll be a society queen.'

The marshal smiled at her credulity. As if he would take her anywhere! He had taken a ride out to the dreary hamlet of Bear Paw mainly to tell Ephraim to keep his mouth shut if anybody started asking questions. Otherwise he might regret it. He had asked about Jan Keerkgarten and, being told he had gone to town for supplies would be away two days, he had called in at his ramshackle farm. He had found his wife, Helga Keerkgarten, baking bread and tending numerous brats and bratlings. When he shooed them out, pushed Helga into the bedroom and shut the latch she knew what he had come for. She did not severely object. The marshal had grappled with her before. She looked forward to his visits as a welcome break to the tedium of life on the farm. The bearded marshal was a handsome and amusing man.

'Will you really take me with you?' She stroked his neatly clipped moustache and beard, and tried to kiss him. 'And the little ones?'

'Hey, hang on. Hold your horses, Helga. I'm spilling this. Sure I'll take you. I'll fill a stagecoach with you all. Old Jan can go hang.'

She giggled and lay her pale-haired head on his bare stomach. That was the view the marshal preferred. He didn't have to look at her stupid face. 'Go on,' he urged her, and pushed her head down as he swigged from the jug.

Plummer wasn't sure why he bothered with her. He could have his pick of the girls back at the saloon, apart from that stuck-up bitch, Susan. But he liked a woman with big lungs and a wide mouth. 'Hey,' he groaned. 'That's nice.' And there was something about having another man's wife. Like stealing the apples on the other side of the fence. They always tasted sweeter.

There was a jingle of a bridle and the shuffle of a horse's hoofs as a rider passed the canvas-covered window of the cabin. Helga stopped what she was doing and peered up through her fronds of white hair, her mouth still wetly open.

Her eyes registered fear. 'It's my husband!'

'I thought you said he was away 'til

tomorrow.' Part of the marshal's anatomy had gone suddenly limp while the rest of him tensed. He reached for his gunbelt hanging from the iron bedstead. 'Shee-it!'

'Here,' she whispered, kneeling up and grabbing at his clothes. 'Get through the window. Please!'

'He's seen my hoss.' The marshal cocked his big Remington revolver. He listened. There was the wail of a child, a bootfall across the outer room, and the wooden door rattled open.

'Helga!' The Norwegian settler's cry was one of dismay and shock as he saw his wife kneeling on the bed, naked, her pendulous breasts swinging, the hairy-chested marshal sprawled beside her. Jan Keerkgarten had his carbine half-raised. 'Get out of my house, you sonuvbitch.'

'Get out of it yourself, you ain't s'posed to be here.' Plummer grabbed Helga's blonde locks, dragged her back across his chest as Jan fired. Helga screamed. The marshal's revolver barked out. When the black cloud of gunsmoke cleared Keerkgarten was lying on his back in a dark pool of blood. Helga was slumped against Plummer, a bloody red hole blasted in her lung. Her blue eyes were fixed on the ceiling.

'Get off of me, you whore,' Plummer snarled, and hurriedly began pulling on his clothes as the children crowded into the bedroom door and stared with awe at their dead parents. Another man appeared behind them. He was a stocky little Irish farmer who lived on a neighbouring patch. He had a shotgun in his hands, the barrel aimed at the marshal.

'I'll take that revolver, Plummer. Drop it, man. I'm taking you in.'

The marshal had laid the revolver aside while he struggled into his pants. There was nothing he could do. The Irishman had the drop on him. 'It was an accident,' he muttered. 'Get out of here or you'll be a dead man, too.'

'I don't think so.' The little Irishman edged forward and retrieved the revolver from the bed. 'These were good people before you came along. Somebody's got to pay for this. Get your boots on, you bastard. I'm making a citizen's arrest.'

The Irishman rode into Bannack City behind Marshal Plummer, his shot-gun aimed at his back. 'Anybody interfere he gets the benefit of both barrels. Plummer's killed Jan Keerkgarten and his wife. There's seven orphaned children. Where's Doc Zabriskie?'

'Here I am,' the doctor said. 'What's happened?'

'Can you handle this? I'm willing to give evidence against him.'

The doctor looked around. Most of the onlookers, rough settlers and miners, seemed hostile to Plummer. Kill a man, maybe, but not when he had seven children. And most of Plummer's cronies were out at the mine, although a few of his roughnecks had come tumbling out of The Montana Dancing Palace. Among them was Fat Alec who came flapping over towards them. 'You've no right, Zabriskie.'

'Citizens' rights. We'll hold a miners' court. We'll get to the bottom of this. Just because he wears a marshal's badge he won't get preferential treatment. March him to his office, men, put him in irons.'

'You–' Plummer began cursing luridly, protesting his innocence, but was pushed roughly away through the throng. He turned and faced Zabriskie. 'Don't think you'll get away with this,' he shouted. But he was dragged on through the mud.

Judge Cyril Smith wobbled into Doc

Zabriskie's surgery, dabbing with a silk handkerchief at his perspiring brow, the thin black hairs clinging to it. 'I've got a writ of habeas corpus. You'll have to release the marshal. There's been a breach of the Bill of Rights involved in his arrest.'

'You can have a writ of hocus pocus for all I care.' Doc Zabriskie went over and kicked the door shut. 'Sit down, elephant arse. And get this straight. Plummer's going to be tried before his peers, that is the citizens of Bannack. And you, as the so-called judge, are going to conduct the trial according to miners' law. I don't want any of your tricks, any habeas corpus, which I doubt you know the meaning of, or any other titifallarkins. You'll just sit there and bring in the verdict of the people, and sentence him, accordingly. You know what the penalty for homicide is, don't you?'

'You trying to railroad me, Doc?' Smith mopped some more at the sweat that rolled from his temples, across his trembling chins and into his collar. 'You know I'll be a dead man if I sentence him to hang.'

'And you might well be if you don't,' Zabriskie said, studying him, meaningfully. 'You understand?'

Shoot was surprised to see the Irishman with the pug face, the one who had spoken out at the Bear Paw saloon, giving evidence. His name was Jerry O'Flanagan, and the packed livery barn fell silent as he described what he had heard and seen. How he had ridden homewards with his friend Keerkgarten. How they had seen the marshal's horse outside the cabin and his friend had said, 'I wonder what he wants?' How he had heard two shots. How he had found his friend dead on the floor, his wife's naked corpse on the bed, the marshal in a state of undress.

'Hang the swine,' a woman's voice in the crowd shouted. 'Think of those poor children. Who's going to look after them now?'

Boon Helm, Joe Pizanthia, Gad Moore, Montana Romaine, and other rough characters, had arrived post haste, and pushed through the crowd to stand in the front row where they glowered at the jury. Judge Smith had insisted they had a jury but had refused several on the grounds of mixed blood. The twelve citizens shuffled uncomfortably under their regard. 'You reckon any one of these would be fool enough to bring in a guilty verdict?' Romaine growled out loud at one point.

'We don't need any more interruptions like that,' Doc Zabriskie said, as he questioned the marshal.

Plummer stood, arrogantly, in his own chains, and smiled at the crowd, especially the ladies. 'Sure I was in her bed. She was hot for me. We didn't expect her damn fool husband would come home. The lunatic fired first, killed his wife. I fired in self-defence. What else do you expect me to do?'

Plummer saw his arrogance wasn't cutting much ice and changed his tactics, pulled out his bandanna and wiped his eyes. 'I don't know what else to say. It's terrible about Helga. I loved her. We were planning to go away. I love those kids. I'll see they're done well by, I promise you that.' He gave a long shuddering snuffle and broke down sobbing into his 'kerchief.

'Are we not reminded, ladies and gentlemen, of a certain scaly, long-toothed reptile that inhabits Florida's glades?' the doctor remarked, amid smiles.

The jury trooped out and trooped back in to say they found Plummer guilty of manslaughter. They strongly recommended mercy. There was a big howl of protest from the miners who were tired of the marshal's card-sharping, womanizing ways.

'Give him as much mercy as he gave the Norwegian,' a woman cried.

Judge Smith trembled like a jelly as he tried to make up his mind. If he went one way ... but on the other hand...? He hardly dared look at Boon or Zabriskie as he banged his gavel and sentenced Plummer to six years in San Quentin prison.

Doc Zabriskie asked that he be escorted there by a civilian armed guard. Helm and his men were causing such a stir he feared they might try to get away with the prisoner there and then. He also asked that a donation be taken up for the deceaseds' family and they tried to find places for the children in suitable homes.

This was agreed with a great cheer and Marshal Plummer was bundled away in chains. As he was put into the stagecoach there were taunts and jeers from numerous men, but also sighs and fluttered handkerchiefs from certain ladies.

Suddenly Plummer's expression changed to one of menace as he leaned from the window of the coach. 'I'll be back,' he shouted. 'And that's when you'll all burn in hell.'

Shoot watched the stagecoach go swinging

away out of town, out on the trail through the Rocky Mountains, a journey of hundreds of miles through desolate territory to Salt Lake City, Utah, the metropolis of the Latter Day Saints, and the connecting railroad to California.

He glanced down the muddy hill and saw the three-storey hotel where Susan had rooms. 'I think I'll go and make a social call,' he muttered. His passion for her was still tearing him apart. He would tell her plainly, either she should consent to be his gal, maybe his wife in a while, or he would go away, leave the territory, head for Colorado, try to rid himself of his obsession. 'I know she likes me. I can see it in her eyes. She just won't admit it, thass all. She's as stubborn as ole Millie the mule.'

The desk clerk gave him a curious look as he stepped past him and up the rickety stairs. He rapped on her door and stood waiting. His heart had begun thudding at the portent of what he was about to say. How come a slip of a girl could scare him more than any man could? He could hear sounds of movement and rapped again, more urgently.

The door opened and Doc Zabriskie stood there, his stocky bulk filling the doorway. He was in shirt sleeves, which were rolled up his brawny arms, and he had his collar off. 'Yes?' He did not seem too friendly.

'Doc!' Shoot was more than surprised to see him. 'What are you doing here?'

'I might ask the same of you.'

'Is something wrong? Is Susan ill?'

'No, her fears are unfounded. I've just concluded my examination.'

Shoot followed him into the room and watched as Zabriskie went over to the jug and wash-stand and bathed his hands. 'Susie,' Zabriskie called. 'You've got a visitor, my dear.'

'Yes.' Shoot heard her voice which was followed by an irritated sigh, and a groan of bedsprings. 'Tell him to wait there.'

'Don't disturb yourself if you're not well,' Shoot called. 'Stay where you are.'

'And you stay where you are. I'll be out in a minute.'

Shoot heard the rustle of clothes and felt somehow uncomfortable as Doc Zabriskie pulled on his silk-backed waistcoat, fiddled with his cufflinks and collar at the mirror, ignoring him. He did not like to ask what the suspected illness was. He guessed it was some womanly thing.

Zabriskie brushed his fringe of grey hair

out of his eyes, put on his butternut suit jacket and went into the bedroom. He emerged with his bag in his hand. 'So long, Susie,' he called. 'Remember what I've told you.' He nodded to Shoot and went out, closing the door firmly behind him.

After a while Susan appeared. She was wearing a white cambric nightdress with an ornate lace collar and silk ribbons, covered decently by a sapphire-blue embroidered dressing-gown. She had white stockings on her feet but was not wearing shoes. Her skin, normally pale, had the effect heightened by a touch of rouge and crimson colour on her lips.

'Yes, what do you want?'

Her tone was not at all friendly. It kinda shattered his resolve. Sometimes it seemed she did not like him at all. Maybe she was just on edge. Nobody liked having to call the doctor in. 'I'm sorry. I didn't know you were ... I didn't mean to intrude ... how are you ... you don't look too well.'

'I'm perfectly fine, thank you, or so the doctor assures me.' Her cheeks coloured up under the artificial colour and her eyes blazed like jewels. 'What do you want? Why are you always spying on me?'

'I'm not spying. I ... I came to ask you if

you'll marry me. I've got to know.'

'Marry you?' She made it sound as if it were the most absurd and distasteful idea in the world. She sat down in the armchair and cupped her head in her hands, her loose tresses tumbling down dark and glossy as a waterfall. Her shoulders began to tremble. At first he thought she was beginning to weep. And then he saw that she was laughing. She raised her face, showing her mouthful of fine white teeth, her pink tongue, gazing at him through her tears, her face contorted with laughter. She lay back in the chair, holding her sides as if they might split, and laughed like the very devil.

'It ain't that funny, is it?'

'I'm sorry.' She was simmering down, but still giving little giggles. 'I shouldn't laugh at you. It was just so ... so ... why should I want to marry you?'

'Because I love you and you love me.'

'Love? Me, love you?' Again it sounded quite absurd. 'What makes you think so? Have I given you any encouragement?'

'No, but–'

'But, even if I did, which I don't, that would be no reason to marry you. I've told you my reasons before. No girl, not one with any sense, marries for love. They marry for position, for security, for – let's say it, that horrible word – cash. Have you any?'

'No, but–' Why tell her about the mine? He did not want to buy her.

'No, but. Oh, really, Shoot, do you really think I'm crazy enough–?'

He grabbed hold of her by her shoulders, he pulled her up to him, and forced his lips upon hers.

'Mmmm...' She was trying to speak, her lips firm and unresponsive as he held her body and head forcibly close to him. Whether it was surprise, or what, she became more relaxed, her lips opening, slightly, as if tasting, testing him, curious. But she was still trying to press him away. His blood was surging through him. He ripped her dressing-gown open, jammed her hard against the wall, and could feel her body warm and shapely beneath the thin nightdress.

She broke her head away from him and gasped for air. 'What the hell do you think you're doing?'

'What do you think I'm doing?' One of his hands held her by the neck. The other was feeling for her bosom. 'I've told you, Susan. I must have you.'

'For Christ's sake, give a girl a chance to breathe.'

He was shocked by the coarseness of her speech. He could not cease. 'If I can't have you, nobody will have you.'

'What, are you going to kill me now?' He saw the scorn in her eyes as she arched up against the wall. 'The brave and gentlemanly Mister Johannson. What are you going to do, rape me first? Hasn't it occurred to you I might scream?'

Shoot put a booted knee between her legs and forcibly manoeuvred her through the door into her bedroom. 'No.' Suddenly he realized the enormity of what he was doing, an act regarded on the frontier as worse than murder. He put her deliberately aside, put his hand to his brow, tried to control his raging emotions, his bodily need. 'I would be no better than an animal. I'm sorry. I'll go. You won't see me again.'

She regarded him with her soulful green eyes, unsure and uncertain. 'Oh, come on, Shoot.' She took his hand in her fingertips and drew him back to the unmade bed. 'If it means so much to you.'

Susan sat down on the bedsheets and began to undo his buttons, poking her icy fingers into him. And he shuddered as he touched her hair and gazed down at her with awe.

‘Are you satisfied now?’ she asked, as he lay half-dressed upon her. ‘Come on, you can’t stay here all day.’

‘Why?’ he muttered, still in a state of bliss to be, miraculously, beside her, holding her. ‘Why not?’

‘Men!’ She heaved him away, indignantly. ‘You’re all the same. Pathetic.’

She went behind the screen and began to wash and dress. She looked over at him, her shoulders bare. ‘Are you still here? Can’t a girl have any privacy? Go on. I said go. Get out of my bed. You’ve had what you came for.’

Shoot stared at her, confused and disconsolate. He hitched his belt tight, savagely; pulled on his jacket. ‘OK, I’m going,’ he said.

‘And don’t think this changes anything,’ she called out, meeting his eyes, unblinking. ‘I’ve still no intention of marrying you. So, don’t go acting like you think I will, if we meet. And don’t go bragging about this. I’ve got a reputation to keep, though you might not think so now.’

‘I wouldn’t think that,’ he said, quietly.

So that was that! She wouldn’t marry him.

She didn't want to be 'some lousy miner's whore'. He didn't blame her. It was the way of the world. 'Grow up. Open your eyes,' he chided himself. All women married for security, more or less. It was a bonus if a man loved and respected her, but nobody wanted to wed some penniless derelict. They needed a man with prospects, a man with at least some hope of keeping her and her children in comfort. No marriage flourished in poverty. Hadn't he seen that in his own parents, forever bickering? Because of what? Money. Or the absence of it. No, he did not blame her. She was right. That was why she had done it to him like that, that disgusting wonderful act. He had never known a woman would do that. She didn't want to have his baby. That was why. How could he blame her? He had practically forced himself upon her. Threatened to kill her. She was probably scared for her life ... although she never looked scared. She seemed incapable of fear. She seemed to have only contempt.

OK, if it means so much to her, he thought, and spoke out loud to Petroleum as they sat in The Hangover Hole. 'We're going to get your mine back.'

'Our mine, boy. It's half yourn. And how

are we going to do that? They've got it guarded heavier than Fort Knox.'

'I'll tell you how. I need that mine, that money. And I'm gonna get it if I die in the attempt. You remember that old howitzer the army abandoned on the edge of town?'

'Indeed I do. We rarely see our blue-belly boys in these wild parts these days. I guess they've got a war to fight. The nearest soldier now would be at Fort Benton. Why, would ye be thinking of selling it back to 'em?'

'No, I'm thinking of borrowing it. We've got plenty of gunpowder. They left a pile of shot. I've seen how those things work. It would be easy enough.'

'Ye're not? Ye're crazy!'

'Crazy, maybe. But it ain't no use sittin' here feeling sorry for ourselves. Come on. I need that mine. It's my future. My marital prospects. The only way. It don't belong to those bastards. You worked hard to reach that seam.'

'Aye and it cost me quite a bit, too. What are we sittin' here for?'

As one accord they ran out, harnessed the piebald to the wagon, went and looked for the howitzer. Yes, it was still in working condition. A trifle rusty, that was all. They loaded up the shot in to the wagon, and hitched the big bay to the gun carriage.

'Forward, men,' Shoot shouted. 'Gee, it's like being back in the war again.'

They trundled up to the barrier across the track to the mine. Several shots whined out and shouts warned them not to approach closer. 'We don't need to approach closer. This gun's got a range of a quarter of a mile,' Shoot yelled.

POW! His first shot missed. He hadn't been trained as a gunner. So did the second. WHUMPH! But the third. POW-EE! One of the gun emplacements went up in a shower of bodies, arms, legs and heads. 'Third time lucky!' he shouted, doing a dance of triumph with his partner.

It didn't matter about showing themselves. Men in the other two gun emplacements jumped out of their holes like frightened rabbits and went bobbing off up the hillside towards the mine shaft.

'This can come down for a start,' Petroleum roared, uprooting the 'Plummer and Helm Mine' placard, tearing the barrier aside.

'No sign of Boon Helm, more's the pity. There don't seem to be so many of them here, Must be out robbin' or card-cheatin' somewhere.'

'There's that greaser. Durned fool's gone into the cabin. Must think it's solid enough to withstand this thing.'

'We'll soon see about that!' Shoot whooped, reloading the cannon as if impervious to the flying bullets coming from the cabin. 'Right!' He lashed his ramrod at the bay. 'Forward, men. Let's get a bit closer. Maybe it will improve my aim.'

They rushed the howitzer up the hill and rolled it into position beside a big rock where they could get cover. Shoot peered over and shouted, 'You men got one last chance to surrender. To get off our land.'

Mexican Joe came to the door of the cabin. 'Go to hell,' he shouted, and loosed off both barrels of his shot-gun.

'Well, he asked for it.' Shoot calmly leaned over and lit the fuse.

He jumped back and covered his ears as the howitzer jerked and roared. KAPOW!

A direct hit. The cabin and those in it were blown to atoms, as if it were some flimsy dolls' house.

'Yeeee-hooo!' Shoot gave a rebel yell, or as he'd heard one from the other side at Bull Run.

'Some of 'em's taken cover in the mine.'

'We'll soon flush 'em out of there.'

They hitched up the cannon again and took it to the top of the hill, ducking down behind the rocks as revolver fire came from the entry to the shaft.

'You men want to be entombed in there?' Shoot hollered. 'We'll give you three seconds then we're going to blow this mine to smithereens.'

There was a pause, and a scared face appeared. And three dusty-clothed men stepped out, their hands in the air.

'Don't shoot,' one pleaded.

'What shall we do with 'em, Mister Jones?'

'Aw, ye varmints can clear off. Ye'd be wise to clear right out of the territory. If we ever see your faces again we'll kill ye, I promise ye.'

'Is it fair to let 'em loose on other unsuspectin' citizens? Shouldn't we hang 'em high?'

But the desperadoes were already hurrying off down the hill. Shoot put a few shots about their ears to keep them moving.

'Well, pardner.' He turned to Petroleum and offered his hand. 'We're back in business.'

A grin split Jones's gunpowder-blackened

face. He looked likc a nigger minstrel. 'We sure are. And don't worry. That filly ain't gonna say no to a cool half-million. Ye're as good as married, son. Yours is gonna be a life of bliss from now on.'

Shoot grinned, grimly, though he wasn't so sure. 'Let's hope so.'

NINE

Wells' and Fargo's overland stage express bumped and swayed up a rough, rugged track making good time five hours out of Bannack City. The driver, Cyrus Skinner, cracked his whip over the backs of the team as they took the strain up the incline to Hell Pass, so called because of the way Bannack Indians used to come charging through it, screaming like devils out of hell. The shotgun guard hung on beside Cyrus and, behind them, were two scruffily clad miners who had decided to try their luck some place else. Inside were a plump widow, Mary Wright, in a poke bonnet bound for Bear Paw, a gaudily dressed goodtime gal known as Weasel-Tooth Alice, who was heading for Nevada in search of richer pickings, Henry Plummer, and the guard with a carbine who had agreed to escort him to Salt Lake and hand him over to a US Marshal with the signed documents of his six-year sentence. The coach rocked back and forth and Plummer, in chains hand and foot, was amusing himself making indecent remarks to the widow and Alice.

'If you don't shut your filthy mouth you'll get the butt of this gun across your head,' the guard growled.

'And I'll sue you,' Plummer smiled, 'for ill-treatment of a prisoner.'

Great eroded cliffs of rock enclosed the pass and the guard on top nervously cocked his shot-gun as he saw two *hombres* walking their horses up the trail before them. The men half-turned in the saddle and doffed their hands to their hats in salute. One had a slain deer slung cross the back of his saddle. They looked like hunters and appeared to pose no threat. The stage creaked and rumbled past them on up through the pass. At a precipitous bend in the trail Cyrus Skinner happened to glance back and saw one of the hunters raise a rifle. A shot cracked out and the guard beside him cried out, momentarily, and pitched from the box, tumbling down into a rocky ravine. At the same time another rifle shot came from the rocks on the canyon side and the off-wheeler went down to be dragged along in a tumult of broken traces and kicking horses, the coach skidding to one side for thirty yards.

'Whoa, you crazy coyotes,' Cyrus yelled, trying to haul in the horses, but the coach lurched, sickeningly, and careered down the bank to come to a bone-shuddering halt jammed against a rock wall. The passengers' screams and cries of dismay as they were hurled about like rag dolls intensified when they saw six dark-clothed and masked riders appear above them through the cloud of dust.

The guard inside fired his carbine and took one of them out of the saddle. One of the miners on top pulled a revolver and blammed away wildly. Incensed, the raiders raised their revolvers and carbines and aimed an ear-shattering volley of lead at the passengers. The two miners on top were cut to pieces, riddled with lead, and the bank guard took the long sleep with a bullet through his brain.

'The rest of you get out of there.' The raider who shouted the command spoke with a husky educated drawl, as if accustomed to being obeyed. 'Hurry up! You, too, Plummer.'

The two females tried to claw and scramble their way out of the wreckage, followed by Plummer in his chains. 'Hey,' he grinned. 'This is real friendly of you to rescue me, boys.'

'Shut up. OK, throw that box down, Skinner. And don't try any monkey tricks or you'll be headed for eternity. You bastards have killed one of my boys. For Christ's sake, somebody put a slug into that horse.'

The lead horse was screaming and thrashing in a tangle of harness, down on the ground, its eyes bulging, as the rest of the team tried to pull away from it. One of the robbers rode over and silenced it with a shell from his sawn-off.

Cyrus Skinner pulled a strongbox from beneath his seat and hurled it to the ground. The masked man with the sawn-off shattered the lock with his second barrel. He gave a whistle of awe as he examined the contents. 'Looks like you were right, Captain.'

'Shut your mouth, you fool. Come on, boys. Get that gold dust into the gunny sacks. You women, if you want to stay healthy, had better hand over your valuables.'

'I've got nothing.' Weasel-Tooth Alice put on an air of innocence. 'Only a few dollars in my purse. You wouldn't take that, sir.'

'Search her.'

Alice screamed and cursed as one of the 'hunters', who had now pulled up a band-anna over his face, gave her a back-hander and ripped up her skirts. He dived his hand down into her drawers and came out with a woollen stocking, bright yellow in colour, stuffed with gold dust. It was tied to a belt around her waist. He tore it away and found another hanging to the other hip.

'I knew this skinny slut didn't have hips that size,' Plummer said, and laughed. 'How about getting these chains off me, boys?'

'What makes you think we've come to help you, Marshal?' The leader, his face swathed in a black mask, with only slits for eyes and mouth, moved his horse forward so that Plummer tumbled backwards to the ground. 'You're staying here. Enjoy your stay in San Quentin. Sorry we won't be able to send you your share of that mine.'

'You son-of-a-bitch.' Plummer looked up, puzzled. 'Is that you–?'

But he quickly decided to say no more as the masked man pointed his revolver at his head.

'I would advise you to keep your mouth shut, Henry. Come along, madam. I can see you're hiding something in your bosom. Get it out, unless you want– The widow quickly tugged a purse from her dress. 'This is really all. You wouldn't...' The 'hunter' snatched it from her and pulled her rings from her fingers as she began to whimper.

'Very wise. Which is more important, your life or your cash? Hurry, boys. We've got a long ride.'

Cyrus Skinner suddenly jumped from the box and made a dash back along the trail. The masked leader turned and fired his big Paterson revolver and Skinner tumbled into the rocks. As he swirled, the blanket that had been draped across his horse's head to camouflage it, was blown aside by the wind. It was revealed as a fine bay gelding with a distinctive star blaze on its nose.

'Come on, let's move,' the leader shouted, and the men climbed on to their mounts and went loping away on up the trail through the pass.

'Boys,' the marshal shouted after them. 'Don't run out on me.'

'What we gonna do now?' Weasel-Tooth Alice wailed.

'You can do what you damn well like. I'm gettin' outa here.' Henry Plummer hopped in his chains over to the dead road agent, released his new Wesson Brothers,* six-gun

* Manufactured prior to the Wessons joining Smith.

from his death grip, and was about to try to shoot through his irons when he paused. 'Hey, what am I doing? The guard's got the key in his pocket. Get it, Alice, and get these chains offen me.'

When the girl had done as he bid, Plummer cut free one of the stage horses. He stuffed the revolver in his belt, picked up the guard's carbine, jumped on the horse's back, and set off up the pass.

'Goodbye, ladies,' he called. 'Give my regards to the good people of Bannack. They're going to regret the day they ever put me in chains.'

'So that's your version of events?'

Judge Cyril Smith was in his office interrogating Cyrus Skinner, backed by a crowd of storekeepers and miners. 'You say you tripped on a stone and when you came to they'd all gone. Along with sixty-two thousand dollars of bullion.'

'And my pokes of gold dust,' Weasel-Tooth Alice said. 'Don't forget that. I want that back.'

'Whooee!' Coal Oil Jim cried. 'How did they know the stage was carrying that much?'

'They knew all right,' Petroleum Jones put

in. 'Ain't it funny that they killed all the other men but let Cyrus and Plummer go free.'

'Hold on,' Skinner protested. 'What you suggestin'?'

'I'm suggestin' this was an inside job. And you certainly knew that bullion would be under your seat.'

'Why you–! What's this? You tryin' to railroad me?'

'Skinner's certainly got a bump on his head,' Judge Smith remarked. 'It tallies with his story.'

'He coulda given himself that little graze,' Petroleum retorted. 'What's the matter with you people? You gonna let them get away with this?'

'Skinner gambled his saloon away,' Ma Payne, the storekeeper, said. 'He's a no-good. I wouldn't put it past him.'

Weasel-Tooth Alice had ridden in with Cyrus on the stage horses to alert the town. 'I've a pretty good idea who's behind this,' she said. 'They called the leader of these road agents, Captain. And it sure sounded like him. I didn't get a look at his face. But I got a look at his horse. A bay with a starlike blaze.

'The same one that fella rode who blew up

my mine and took a pot-shot at me,' Petroleum said. 'I say we ride out to the captain's farm and see what's going on. You say there were five of 'em? Who's ready to take these outlaws on?'

'Just a minute.' Judge Smith tried to calm the uproar of men volunteering to ride. 'This is ridiculous. The captain's a respectable man. It's his stage that's been robbed. Don't let's get carried away.'

'It's him who's carried it away,' Petroleum roared. 'The bullion he's supposed to guard.'

Shoot had been listening intently. 'What about Plummer? Shouldn't we go after him?'

'We'll do that,' Petroleum shouted, 'after we've got the captain.'

The men cheered and hurried to load their weapons, rustle up provisions for the long ride, and saddle their horses. The excitement in the air was electric. There was nothing like a manhunt.

Dusk was drawing in as ex-Marshal Plummer pounded along the trail. Caution had made him by-pass Bear Paw where the stage would have had a change of horses. His own mount was blowing hard and flagging badly. It couldn't go much further. He wanted to get right away before they came after him. There would be time enough to get himself a gang of gunmen together to return to take his revenge on Bannack City. He had seen no sign of the road agents. They must have cast off the trail. He needed to keep riding through the night if he was to make his getaway. But, if he did that this beast would surely die under him.

It was then that he spied an encampment of brushwood and skin Indian dwellings among some windbent trees. He tightened his grip on the carbine and rode in to them. Some curs came snarling and yapping towards him and a couple of squaws and a gaggle of children looked up at his approach. They were a weatherbeaten, dishevelled group, two families at the most. Bannacks. Plummer was not afraid of them. They had had the fight beaten out of them long ago. They squatted in the dust as miserable as their curs.

'Where's your chief?' Plummer asked, stepping down.

A white-haired grandfather stepped out of one of the wickyups. 'What you want, Marshal?' he said. 'We done nothing wrong.'

'I'm hungry. You got anything to eat and drink?'

The old chief was bowed with age, his fringed buckskins worn and ill-fitting, his face furrowed by deep lines, but he held his head proudly, and indicated the squaws should serve from the stewpot. They did so and Plummer squatted and gobbled the mess down.

He tossed the wooden plate aside without thanks, with a white man's arrogance, and eyed them. 'I need a horse. You got one over there. I'll exchange it for mine.'

The chief went to look at Plummer's sweated-up horse and shook his head. 'This horse no good. This coach horse. Men come and say I stole it. No deal, Marshal.'

'I tell you it's mine, you dumb savage. What you trying to say, I stole it? I'll give you a receipt if you like.' He picked up his carbine and strode over to the hobbled pinto. 'I'm taking this.'

'No! That our horse. That good horse.' The chief went after him and grabbed his arm. 'We need this horse.'

Plummer clubbed him to the ground with the carbine, put the barrel to his brow and blew the chiefs head apart like a splattered melon. The squaws started screaming as they saw the chief's blood pouring into the dust. A young boy ran at Plummer brandishing a tomahawk. Plummer produced the Wesson revolver and shot him through the chest. The boy toppled down beside the chief; Plummer climbed on to the pinto and kicked his heels into its sides. A squaw tried to hang on to his leg. He shot her point blank in the face, and galloped back to the trail.

Not so many men turned up to join the posse of Bannack City vigilantes as had at first been fired with righteousness. Some had had second thoughts as to their safety and the captain's influence in the territory. Others had remembered urgent work to do at their claims. But twelve men led by Shoot Johannson, Petroleum Jones, and Jack Brady, who ran a tobacconist's and billiards hall, but had gotten tired of paying protection money, set off at dawn, on the long journey to Bear Paw. Doc Zabriskie was nowhere to be found. He had probably returned to Virginia City, someone said.

When they reached the wreckage of the stage coach they took a look at the two dead guards and two miners, and at the body of one of the roadsters.

'Anybody know him?'

'I seen him about. The usual kinda drifter.

Went by the name of Brown or Smith, maybe. One of the alias tribe, you might say,' Brady remarked. 'Looks like the ravens already made a start on his innards. We'd better bury these boys.'

They scraped out shallow graves and piled rocks on top. Brady took off his top hat, held it over his heart, and looked up at the clouds. 'Life is brief, and death an eternity, oh Lord. It's up to You now what You do with their souls. If You take my advice it's four upstairs and one down below.' He replaced his hat. 'C'mon, let's git.'

At Bear Paw they were joined by the Irishman, Jerry O'Flanagan, who led them out to Slade's ranch. It was already dusk by that time and they approached with caution, leaving their horses, and going on foot, weapons at the ready, along a creek of willows that led to his big log house and the corrals. Petroleum pushed open the door of a barn and pointed to a gelding in a stall. 'There it be, boys. That's his horse. See that blaze?'

A man came into the barn bearing two buckets. 'What'n hell you want?'

'We want a word with Cap'n Slade,' Brady said. 'We've come to arrest him.'

'He ain't here. He's been away at Viginny City all week.'

'Oh, yeah? Huccome this hoss was seen bein' ridden by him when the stage was attacked yesterday? Don't play innocent with us. Where's the rest of the gang? They in the house?'

'There ain't nobody but me and a coupla ranch hands. I got the chickens, hosses and milch cows to feed so outa my way.'

Brady grabbed him as he tried to push by. 'You sayin' this hoss was in its stall late afternoon yesterday?'

'No. That's an odd thing,' the man said. 'Star was gone when I looked in. I thought maybe he'd got loose or been stolen. Then after dark he was back here again and all sweated up.'

'That's good enough for us,' Petroleum yelled. 'Let's go question them two hands and take a look in the house.'

'You cain't go bustin' in there–'

'You try stop us,' Brady muttered, 'your heels will be swinging two feet off the ground. Same as Slade's will when we catch him.'

The two boys in the bunkhouse didn't put up any resistance and gave the same story. The posse let them go and headed for the log house. It was well appointed, with polished furnishings and lamps and fur rugs on the wooden floors. Brady and his men broke open an escritoire, trunks, a wardrobe, and cupboards. They scattered papers. They looked under the bed, and prised up the floorboards. But they could find no missing bullion.

'You sure made a mess,' the stable hand whined. 'What's the cap'n goin' to say?'

Brady looked a trifle flummoxed. He wiped his perspiring red face and tried to put the lid of the escritoire back, but it clattered to the floor. 'We're wastin' our time, boys. They musta buried it. Or they're headed outa the Territory by now. Well, I got a business to run. I'm goin' back to Bannack City. We'll issue a warrant for his arrest.'

Most of the posse decided to return with him. Shoot and O'Flanagan said they'd follow the mail road on and take a look for Plummer. Petroleum reckoned he ought to get back to hold the mine.

'If we catch him, Jerry here's offered to escort him on to Salt Lake City,' Shoot said. 'So we'd better give him the court papers.

'So long,' Brady called. 'Watch your backs for thet rattlesnake.'

'Sure would have been a durned lot easier if we'd strung him up back at Bannack City,'

O'Flanagan said.

They listened to the wailing of the squaws of the small Bannack tribe as they mourned the loss of their chief, his daughter and grandson, and heard how Plummer had shot them down.

Shoot and Jerry rode on along the mail road which wound its way up towards the Central Divide, a fierce blizzard sweeping down from the icy fangs of the mountains. They pulled down their hats, raised their bandannas, and hunched their shoulders against the blast. It was hard going.

Darkness fell and they came upon a small cabin used by roadmenders but deserted now. As conditions were so icy and treacherous they decided to stay there the night. 'I reckon the varmint's got a thirty-mile lead on us,' Jerry said, as he lit the tin stove with kindling left by the last occupant. 'That's if he's taken this trail.'

'We'll get him,' Shoot said, and searched in his bag for the bacon. 'Don't worry.'

'You think so?' There was a blast of cold air as the door was pushed open. They froze as they heard Plummer's ironic drawl. 'Those could be your famous last words.'

'Where'n hell did you spring from?' Jerry turned and slowly raised his hands as he looked into the unwavering barrel of Plummer's Wesson. Shoot followed suit for he'd laid his guns aside.

'That damn Injun pinto put his foot in a foxhole, threw me. Broke his leg. I had to slit his throat. So, gentlemen, I walked back to this shelter for the night.' Apart from needing a shave and his gambler's fancy clothes somewhat torn and dusty, Plummer had lost none of his arrogance. 'Just as well I did. For now I can borrow your horses. No, don't try anything! How kind of you to light the stove and prepare me a meal. Perhaps you'd both like to step outside? I don't want you stinking up my sleeping-quarters, do I?'

Shoot hesitated, but there was little he could do. Plummer had his revolver in his right hand and the carbine aimed under his left arm. There was every chance he could kill them both if they tried to rush him. By the savage scowl on his countenance he had every intention of so doing.

'Get outside.' Plummer kept a good couple of paces away, edging around them so they were facing away from him. 'And keep your hands high.'

Shoot's hesitation had cost him dear. Maybe he could make a run for it into the darkness? But he was without his guns and Plummer would undoubtedly shoot him in the back. Shoot waited to feel the explosion in his flesh and for his life to be blasted out of him.

'I shoulda done this a long time ago,' Plummer snarled. 'Stand over by them rocks.'

They stepped across the road to the rocks. Shoot heard a hissing sound, as of something flying through the air, and an explosion behind him as Plummer took a sharp intake of breath. When Shoot looked around Plummer was writhing on the ground, an arrow embedded in his shoulder.

Shoot kicked Plummer's weapons away from him and looked up at the trail illumined in the darkness by a trickling carpet of hailstones. Out of the darkness came riding an Indian. It was Five Owls and he had a bow in his hands.

'Phew!' Shoot grinned up at the Bannack. 'That was a tight thing. Many thanks, my friend. You rescued me once again.'

Five Owls jumped lightly down in his moccasins. 'I been trailin' him.'

'Where's your Sharps?'

'Ah!' Five Owls brandished the bow. 'For hunting men I prefer this. It silent.'

'For Christ's sake do somethun,' Plummer moaned. 'Git this arrow outa me.'

Five Owls grabbed him by his hair and raised his knife. 'You kill my family. I kill you now.'

'Since when's it against the law to kill an Injun?' Plummer said, contemptuously. 'You ain't gonna let him, boys. I'm your prisoner.'

Shoot shrugged. 'That's up to Five Owls. Whatever happens, Plummer, you're gonna pay for that massacre of innocents.'

Five Owls glanced at Shoot, his knife poised over the fallen marshal's neck. He pushed him aside, with a sickened expression. 'What he say is right. Nobody care he kill Indian. Me kill lawman many white men come kill many Indian. What you do with him?'

'He is going to prison for many years. I guess we'll get this arrow out. My friend here will take him. Got your rope, Jerry? Make sure you tie him tight.'

'What, around his neck and to the nearest pine?'

'No. I'd like to see him hang as much as you. But I guess we've gotta do what the jury decided. It's time to start living by the law.'

Five Owls watched them doctor Plummer as he warmed himself at the fire and ate with them. He lay down on the floor to sleep awhile. In the morning he had gone.

O'Flanagan put a noose around Plummer's neck, and tied his wrists behind him. 'You're gonna have a long walk, marshal. You reckon you can make it?' He swung on to his horse and gave a jerk of the rope. 'Come on, let's see. It ain't no skin off my nose if you die before we get there.'

Shoot turned back towards Bannack City. When he paused and turned Jerry was climbing up towards the high mountains, Plummer staggering along behind him. If they covered thirty or forty miles a day it was going to be a long journey all the way across Wyoming to Utah.

On his way back, Shoot called in at Bear Paw and spoke to Widow Wright. Was there anything to identify the robbers? No; like a clucking hen, she just went on about her stolen purse, a beaded one she had bought from a Bannack Indian, and the twenty golden eagles in it, her life savings, and her rosary. 'There was one thing,' she cried. 'The leader carried a big old Paterson revolver.'

Captain Slade had an alibi. He had been in Virginia City on the day of the robbery. Mayor Castner vouched for that. It was all mighty peculiar.

Shoot returned to working on the mine as the days gradually grew warmer. He and Petroleum hauled out a wagonload of the galena rock and presented it to the honest assayer, who, with the sudden departure of Parsnip Sessions, had set up an office in Bannack City. He gave them a cheque for $5,000 as down payment to draw on his account in Salt Lake City.

'Whee-hoo!' Petroleum yelled, as they headed for The Hangover Hole. 'I know this is only a bit of paper but we're rich, boy.'

Shoot spruced himself up and went to look for Susan at the Montana Arcade. She was not among the hurdy-gurdy gals. So he slugged back another rum and walked along to her rooming-house.

She was statuesque in a dress of rustling green silk as she opened the door, her eyes reflecting its colour, her neck and shoulders bare, the low-cut dress revealing the valley of her shadowy bosom. 'Well, I never,' she said, and gave him a faint smile. 'I was just about to step out.'

'Can I come in for a few minutes first?'

'Why not?' She stepped aside and ushered him in, and he was taking her in his arms. 'Such ardour! This is a surprise.'

She didn't say a lot more because she was responding, her mouth opening to his kisses, her tongue sliding into his mouth, her body warm and soft against his. And, pretty soon, he had her back on the bed, was pushing up her voluminous frills and furbelows, his roughened hands stroking her thighs in her lacy pantalets. As she lay back and gripped him hard around his neck she whispered in his ear, 'I hear your mine's paying out. Isn't that wonderful?'

Susan gave herself a glance in the mirror as she straightened her clothes, her face flushed from the exercise. Her delicate condition had not yet begun to really show, although Doc Zabriskie had assured her she was three months pregnant. Maybe she should marry Shoot after all? He was young and tall and handsome and somewhat naive. She would have little trouble twisting him round her finger for he was besotted with her. And it hardly mattered about making love to him now for being with child she had no need of birth control! If only *he* did not find out, the child's father.

'There is another man,' she said, as she patted powder to her cheeks and rearranged her hair. 'That's why, before, I couldn't...'

'But now I'm likely to get rich you can?' Shoot lay on the bed and watched her before the mirror as she tied up her plaits. 'Is that it?'

'He will never let me go.' Susan turned to Shoot, her eyes as deep and fathomless as the sea. 'He forced me to be his mistress. He is a powerful man. He will kill me. He will kill you, unless...'

'Unless I kill him first?'

Susan bit her lip and nodded, meaningfully. 'There's no other way, Shoot.'

'You mean that?' Shoot's heart had started thudding. 'Who is he?'

Susan stared at him and shook her head. 'No one you know. No one important. I mean I can't tell you. I daren't. I shouldn't have said anything. Oh, God! Why do men always think they can own me?' Perhaps it's best I don't see you again?'

That suggestion made Shoot's heart thud even faster. He sprang up and shook her by the shoulders. 'I don't care who he is. I don't want to pick a quarrel with him. I've had enough of fighting. But, by God, if he tries to take you away from me, I will, I'll kill him.'

After all, he thought, I've killed plenty of other men. One more won't make much difference. And he can't be much of a man if he treats her in this fashion.'

'Is it Captain Slade?' he demanded.

'No!' She shook her head, avoiding his eyes. 'Don't start about *him* again. Promise me you won't do anything ... unless you have to.'

What does it matter? she thought. If it comes to a duel and one is slain I can still marry the victor. It is a sure bet either way.

TEN

News filtered through to Bannack City in mid-June that Marshal Henry Plummer had been released after only six weeks in San Quentin prison. Several prominent citizens in Montana Territory had signed a petition pleading on his behalf. No doubt they were in some way indebted to him. And the authorities had decided there were irregularities at his trial, his rights as a citizen had been ignored.

'What about the rights of those he murdered?' Doc Zabriskie fumed. 'There's a nasty smell here. There's been no presidential pardon. I reckon he paid off the governor with his share from that bullion robbery, or whatever.'

Zabriskie had found Shoot at the Montana Arcade. The card playing and dancing was in full swing, the girls whooping, the orchestra crashing out its cadences. Zabriskie seemed very bet-up about the news. His broad shoulders tight against the butternut suiting, he sat there and glowered through his grey beard and fringe.

'News is,' he said, 'that he's getting Boon Helm and his old gang back together. That he's heading back to take vengeance on all those who spoke against him at his trial.'

Shoot watched Susan being swung around by some horny old-timer in a battered hat. He had told her she didn't need to be a hurdy-gurdy any more, but she had replied that she wished to be independent until such time as she was wed, and, anyway, she enjoyed the dancing.

Shoot, rich only in paper money, and with a limited amount of gold coin at his disposal, had asked *when* they were going to be married? Why not immediately? But she had fobbed him off. 'It's not easy. There's this other man. He's threatened me.'

Shoot returned his attention to Zabriskie. 'Surely folks wouldn't let Plummer cause any trouble?'

'How they gonna stop him? Already some of the ruffians who used to ride with him have drifted back into town. The only thing to do is hang a few of 'em so they don't get the chance to join him.'

'Like who?'

'Like Gad Moore for a start. He stuck his knife in an unarmed Dutchman over a small bet. He's one of Plummer's guns. The committee have him marked. Will you join us now?'

'Maybe.'

Shoot went to the bar for another beer. When he turned, and put the foaming flagon to his lips, he saw Doc Zabriskie dancing with Susan. It was the latest craze from Europe, an Austrian polka. As they swirled round and round, back and forth, they appeared to be deep in conversation. A worm of jealousy wriggled in Shoot. What could they be talking about? She rarely spoke to *him* so ardently. Oh, well, he shrugged, and swallowed the beer. Guess they're discussing the state of her health or somethun'.

The mud of Bannack City main street had finally hardened over revealing the luckless carcasses of a horse and a mule which had succumbed in its swamp. Shoot had heard a commotion outside the Montana saloon and ambled outside to see what was happening. Gad Moore was being led up the hill by a gang of men led by Doc Zabriskie.

'We're gonna try him for the murder of Dutch Schulz,' Doc shouted as he led them into the livery barn. 'We don't need no damn Judge Smith.'

'Ain't he actin' a bit high-handed?' Shoot muttered to Petroleum. 'This ain't a trial. It's a lynch mob.'

'Seems to me the doc's real worried about Marshal Plummer and Boon Helm coming back,' Petroleum said. 'He aims to wipe out any possible support.'

The trial was briefly pithy. By a show of hands Gad Moore was condemned. Moore, a big muscular giant, grinned and waved to the crowd. He had a saddleback nose, a receding brow and wide gaps between his teeth, symptoms of congenital syphilis. If so, his body would be covered in gaping sores. He did not seem to comprehend that his life was at stake. 'Give me a few days to write to my aunt in Ohio,' he said, cheerfully.

'We'll give you as much time as you gave Dutch Schulz,' Zabriskie said. 'Get a rope, boys.'

'I'm innocent. Dutch cheated. I had to shoot him. Wouldn't you?'

'What about all the others?' Zabriskie thundered. 'I'll write to your aunt, tell her you died a scoundrel on the gallows. Sling the rope over that beam. Start climbing that ladder, Gad.'

Gad did as he was bid, climbing up to the hayloft, the noose around his neck. Zabriskie, himself, tightened it and tied it to the ironwork of a stall in the barn. 'That comfortable enough, Gad?'

'I ain't never been hung afore,' Gad said, grinning goofily. 'What do I do – jump or slide?'

Some of the onlookers in the barn, in spite of the seriousness of the occasion, began to giggle at this remark. Indeed, it was repeated in the city saloons in various versions for days to come.

'Please yourself, Gad,' Zabriskie said. 'But make it snappy. I've a surgery at six.'

The ladder was pulled away so Gad had no alternative but to jump. He pitched himself off, and his face contorted as he kicked and struggled for three or four minutes. The rope was not new and had half-snapped with his weight, until he was suspended by only one strand. The crowd of onlookers held their breath. The last strand broke and Gad slammed to the mud floor. Finally, Doc Zabriskie pronounced life extinct.

'I'll pay for his burial,' he said. 'All right, folks, it's over now.'

Shoot stood staring at the body of Gad. He was not sure he cared for summary justice like this.

'I guess it's the only way,' he said.

Zabriskie certainly was a hard man.

Once the hanging had started it was as if a bloodlust gripped the populace. The vigilante committee rode about the territory, thirty strong, silent men in masks, picking up all suspected miscreants, executing them with the twang of a rope. Cyrus Skinner was one of the first to go. Zabriskie vowed Skinner had passed on information to the road agents.

'Roadster, fence and spy,' was scrawled on a torn piece of cardboard attached to his body as he swung in the breeze.

Marshal Plummer was a man of his word. He rode back into Bannack City one morning at the head of his gang. Boon Helm and Montana Romaine, his lieutenants, at his side as a blood-red dawn rose. His twenty desperadoes were carrying flickering tar-brands in their hands. They charged into the town firing wildly at all and sundry, anyone who happened to be abroad, men, women or children. Ma Payne was loading her churns of milk when a bullet caught her in the throat. Boon Helm galloped up to Coal Oil Jim's store and tossed his torch, shattering the window. The building went up like a bomb.

The Montana badmen howled and yelled and soon flames were licking up the sides of the tinder-dry false-fronts built side by side. Brady leaned from his bedroom above his billiards hall in his nightshirt, a rifle in his hands. A bullet plunged into his belly and he tumbled out on to the canopy and splashed down into a horse trough.

They didn't have it all their own way. The traders and miners had been expecting trouble and slept with shot-guns under their pillows. They were soon at their windows blazing away at the rough-riders below. Flames and smoke engulfed the town as the attackers rode along the sidewalks or charged their horses into stores causing chaos. But many of them paid the price.

Shoot was at the mine when he heard the sound of gunfire. He leaped on the big bay and went riding pell-mell into town. Most of Main Street was a holocaust of fire. Prostitutes were leaping from the Montana Arcade upstairs windows, their dresses and hair aflame. His only thought was for Susan. His mount refused to enter the area of fire, shrieking and rearing. Shoot secured and abandoned her and ran on foot through the burning buildings, as timber fronts crashed down about him. He raised his Colt and fired at any man on horseback who came thudding through the smoke and sparks. Four of them pitched from their saddles from his lead.

He reached the rooming-house and, as he did so, he saw Doc Zabriskie stepping out, a gun in his hand, his broad arm around Susan as she hung on to a carpet bag and huddled into him, a look of terror on her face. 'Are you all right?' Shoot shouted as he saw them.

But, as Susan and Zabriskie stared at him, a strange frozen look on their faces, Shoot saw Boon Helm on horseback cantering, out of the smoke and confusion. He had a carbine gripped to his shoulder and his dark-bearded face was fixed with hatred as he aimed at Zabriskie. His bullet thudded into the woodwork. Shoot fired, wildly. Boon's horse went down, a slug in its chest, kicking as it lay on the hardened mud. Boon Helm had a leg trapped beneath it, an agonized look on his face.

As Zabriskie hurried Susan away, firing a revolver as he went, Shoot saw Marshal Plummer in the midst of it all, wheeling his horse, a crazed, bitter grin on his handsome saturnine features. Plummer looked about him, waving his Wesson revolver, but most of his men were dead or dispersed. He kicked spurs into his mount, gave a wild bloodthirsty yell, and went galloping out of town.

Shoot ran to the end of the blazing buildings where he had left the bay. He leaped on her back and sent her chasing after Plummer. For a mile he raced until he saw a glimpse of the marshal. The skirts of Plummer's frock coat were flailing as he slashed at his mount with a quirt from side to side. Just as well Shoot had caught sight of him, for Plummer veered into a side cut-off that led to Washoe. Shoot followed and ducked down low over his bay's neck as they pounded beneath the branches of trees. He went leaping and splashing through a stream, and out on to Frenchman's Flats. Now it was a straightforward race. Plummer wasn't far ahead, and the bay was gradually gaining. Shoot had one last bullet in his Navy. He was twenty yards behind Plummer when he fired. And missed! Shoot spurred his snorting and spittle-streaming bay to a last effort. He galloped alongside Plummer, loosened his boots from the stirrups, and leaped at him, dragging him across his horse's back and out of the saddle. The air was knocked out of both of them as they hit the mud.

Shoot was the first on his feet, and ran to the marshal as he staggered to his knees. He slammed a hard right hook into his jaw that sent him spinning. Plummer kicked up his boot as Shoot dived on him, and they went rolling over and over, fighting for life. Plummer had his thumbs pressed into Shoot's throat. Shoot knee'd him in the gut and broke his hold. He shot a vicious left into the marshal's fancy waistcoat, and smashed another right into his face ... the marshal was on one knee, panting for breath, his face a mess. He had had enough.

'Where the hell you come from?' he gasped. 'Why'd you come to this Territory? You let me go, I'll make you rich.'

'It's you shouldn't have come back.' Shoot whistled for his horse and roped Plummer. 'I don't need your stolen money. I work hard for mine. Get on that cayuse. We're goin' back to Bannack.'

The girls and citizens standing about in the steaming ashes of Bannack City looked a blackened and bedraggled lot of chickens who'd had their coops burned down around them.

'First things first,' Doc Zabriskie said. 'There's going to be some hangings. Then we'll set to and rebuild this city.'

He seemed oddly off hand with Shoot. 'Hand over that prisoner, Johannson. Don't argue. We don't need no trial. We all know who's behind this.'

Henry Plummer was dishevelled but defiant. 'I told you I'd see you all burn in hell. You touch me and it will be even worse for you. You'll wish you never existed.'

Boon Helm gave a twisted grin as he was hauled up beside him. 'One thing for you, Henry, you never give in. Who you tryin' to kid? We've made a hash of things.'

There wasn't much left standing to toss a rope over. They walked the prisoners to a skeleton of a building being put up on the edge of town, slung two ropes over one of its roof timbers. 'How we goin' to do it, Captain?' Bob Zachary asked as he arranged the nooses around their necks.

Shoot's ears pricked up at the word. He wondered *who* Zachary was calling Captain. And realized that Zachary was one of the vigilante committee and he was addressing Zabriskie as their 'captain'. He saw Susan standing at the back of the crowd watching and he remembered how the Doc had had his coat off when he called on her. Fair enough, if he was doing an examination, but did he need to have his collar off, too?

No, he thought, I'm imagining things.

'Stand 'em on those boxes, boys. Now I'm giving you one last chance of freedom, Marshal. Tell us where that bullion is,' Doc Zabriskie called. 'Tell us who you were in with. Was it Slade?'

'You know I had nothing to do with that robbery. How could I? I was in chains. In my opinion I shouldn't be surprised...'

Zabriskie pulled his revolver and began firing at the box before Plummer could say any more. The men about him joined in, shattering both boxes. Boon Helm gave a last venomous look at Zabriskie and yelled, 'See ya in hell, Doc. We'll be waitin' for ya.'

The ropes twanged taut and the breath of life was choked out of the two men as they swung, their heads falling to one side, their eyes bulging. It was over ... or nearly.

The citizens clustered about the hanged men, wanting to get into the picture an itinerant photographer was setting up. 'Smile, ladies and gents,' he called. 'This is a historic occasion, the hanging of a marshal and his best friend.'

Shoot strode over to Susan, and put an arm around her. She was shivering, her face pale. 'He likes hangings, doesn't he?'

'Who?'

'Paul – Zabriskie.'

'They all do,' Shoot said. 'You'd better come and stay at the cabin.'

He helped her away, lifted her and her heavy bag, on to the horse. When they got to the cabin they found Petroleum Jones had snored through it all.

'What in Hades,' he hooted. 'Why dincha wake me? Ye mean to say I missed all the fun?'

Susan was on her hands and knees sorting out her hastily gathered personal belongings rescued from the rooming-house, taking them from her carpet bag, dresses, stays, pantalets, necklaces, ear bobs, a rag doll, rouge, a silver candlestick, pamphlets, papers, silver dollars, treasury notes, a haphazard jumble of feminine trinkets...

Shoot stepped into the cabin from tending to the horses. 'Jeez,' he joked. 'I thought that bag was heavy. Looks like you got the Bank of America in there.' And he caught sight of a purse beaded like a Bannack Indian moccasin with an eagle design.

'What's this?' He snatched it up and opened the clip. It contained gold coin and – he drew it out with a whistle of surprise – a rosary. 'Widow Wright might be interested to see this.'

There was alarm and guilt in Susan's eyes as she looked up and tried to hastily cover with a blouse something else. Shoot pulled the blouse away to reveal two bright yellow stockings packed with gold dust, some of it trickling out through a hole.

'Leave it alone!' Susan cried, struggling with him. 'It's mine.'

'It looks more like Weasel-Tooth Alice's. Where did you get this? Who gave it you?'

'That's none of your business.' She flared up trying to wrest her wrist from his hand. 'Don't you see, Shoot? We've got to get as much as we can from this Territory and go.

'Even if it's others' property? Tell me!' He shook her by her wrist. 'Was it Zabriskie? You are his mistress, aren't you?'

'No!' Her shout was almost a scream as she shook herself free. 'I'm not his mistress, you fool.'

'He had been in bed with you, hadn't he? That first afternoon before you went with me? Why else should he have had his collar off? Sure, I'm a fool. I didn't want to admit it. And you must have been with him all last night.'

'Why don't you kill him?' she hissed, as she heard the sound of horsemen outside. 'We could have everything.'

Shoot's hand went to his revolver. Too late. Montana Romaine's bulk filled the doorway. And he had a shot-gun levelled at Shoot.

'I'll take that. Easy now.'

Shoot reluctantly surrendered his revolver. He stepped outside and saw that the unarmed Petroleum was there covered by the guns of Bob Zachary, and of Doc Zabriskie, who sat his horse, his ancient revolver in his paw. A Paterson!

'I've come for my wife,' Zabriskie roared.

'Your *wife?*'

'Yes, come over here.' As Susan stepped, hesitantly, towards him, he leaned down and smacked her hard across the face with his gloved hand. 'You double-crossing bitch. Thought you could get him to kill me?'

She lay on the hardened mud, a trickle of blood coming from her lip. 'I didn't, Paul.'

Zabriskie ignored her and studied Shoot and Petroleum with his 'honest' hazel eyes. 'As captain of the Virginia City Vigilante Committee I hereby order your arrest and execution. Is that agreed, boys?'

Montana and Zachary muttered, 'Aye', and gave slight smiles. 'We've brought our own rope, Zachary said. 'It ain't gonna cost you nuthin'.'

'On what grounds?' Petroleum protested. He hadn't caught up with what was happening yet.

'On the grounds that he's a lying crook,' Shoot said. 'Don't you see? Zabriskie was the man behind the bullion robbery. He's probably got it salted away somewhere.'

'On the grounds,' Zabriskie shouted, 'that you both murdered several men with a howitzer in claim-jumping this mine.'

Montana pulled out a notice from his coat on which was scrawled in red paint, 'Murderers and Claim-Jumpers'. He watched Zachary snake two noosed ropes over the bough of a nearby pine, and grinned. 'This is gonna be your epitaph.'

'This mine was stolen from us,' Petroleum said. 'We was gettin' back our rightful property.'

'No. By miners' law this was the Plummer-Helm mine. You had forfeited right to it.' Zabriskie took a document from his pocket. 'I happen to be the chairman of the company.'

'So that's why you were quick to have Boon and Plummer hanged,' Shoot said. 'Don't you two fools see? He got rid of them, same as he did Cyrus Skinner, who used to supply him with information. Same as the others in the gang so they couldn't testify against him. He'll do the same to you. You think he'll let you live?'

'What's he saying?' Montana eyed Zachary, uneasily.

'Get under that pine the both of you,' Doc Zabriskie ordered Shoot and his partner. 'Don't take any notice of him, boys. He's trying to discountenance us. You'll get your share as planned.'

'An *educated* voice,' Shoot muttered. 'I shoulda thought. And there was me blaming Slade for the robbery.'

'Move,' Montana growled at him, jabbing him with the shot-gun. 'Get under that bough.'

Shoot and Petroleum could do little but comply. It was not a very pleasant sensation to feel the hair hempen noose tightened against their throats.

'So long, youngster,' Petroleum said. 'See ye the other side, maybe.'

'Get up on those rocks,' Zachary shouted. 'And when I say jump, you jump.'

'No!' Susan screamed and tried to run to them but Montana held her back. 'Shoot, I didn't want this.'

'Get on with it, Zachary,' Zabriskie ordered, covering them with the Peterson.

'He's just as likely goin' to shoot you two when we're gone.'

'That's the last remark you'll ever make in this world,' Zabriskie said.

But, he spun his horse around with alarm as a bunch of riders came charging up to the mine. They were led by Captain Slade, who had Mayor Joe Castner by his side. 'What's going on here?' Slade demanded.

'We're having a hanging,' Doc Zabriskie bluffed. 'By order of the vigilantes.'

'There'll be a trial first. Surrender your gun, man. And you other two. This is the new citizens' committee and I'm leading it,' Slade said. 'And arrest that woman, too.'

Susan wept and pleaded. 'James,' she said, clutching at his jacket, 'doesn't our relationship mean anything?'

'What relationship?' Slade snorted with indignation. 'With an adulteress and whore, a thief, and accessory to murders? Put them all in irons.'

The citizens of Bannack had too much to do

to bother with a trial. They were busy rescuing what property they could from the ruins of the buildings and making themselves temporary accommodation in tents and wagons. Doc Zabriskie and Susan were padlocked in a cabin while witnesses were brought to testify.

'I'm a new man these days,' Captain Slade said when he met Shoot in the street. 'I've given up the whiskey for good. There'll be no more incidents like at Bear Paw. It's thanks to you, young fellow. The words you said to me made me see my folly.'

'What's going to happen to them, Captain?'

'Ah!' he said, stroking his moustache. 'You were keen on her, weren't you? Don't worry. I don't think it will come to a hanging. Nobody wants to see a young woman strung up.'

'I guess Zabriskie had the perfect cover. Nobody suspected him.'

'No, but he tried to throw suspicion on me, stealing my horse. And some believed him.' He gave Shoot a mock severe regard. 'If I hadn't been at Virginia City at the time of the hold-up I probably wouldn't be alive now.'

Zabriskie gave evidence at his trial stoutly denying all charges, as did Susan. Folk had got so used to the 'honest doctor' that they could hardly believe he could have been behind a murdering gang of road agents.

Many a tear slipped from women's eyes as they heard Susan coolly tell the crowded court, 'Paul was too good-hearted to charge fees for his doctoring to the poor. We couldn't live on his salary. That's why I worked in the dance palace to make ends meet. Of course, he couldn't admit we were married then. It would have been socially impossible.'

Shoot gazed at her, so beautiful and haughty and indomitable she looked and, at the same time so modest in her black silk and white lace collar, her dark hair pulled demurely back. He had to swallow a lump in his throat. He almost half-believed her.

'Don't let her fool ye,' Petroleum whispered, huskily. 'That little bitch is so obsessed by riches she probably nagged a once-good man, a one-time decent leader of the vigilantes into abusing his position. In my opinion she corrupted Doc Zabriskie.'

The verdict of the jury, presided over by Joe Castner, was that they should be banished from the Territory forthwith, given three days to attend to their affairs.

As she was bustled out of the court room on Zabriskie's arm, Susan glanced at Shoot and she gave him a triumphant smile. But the green eyes behind the long black lashes contained simultaneously, a wild pain, as if she were still a captive creature.

'They've probably got that bullion waiting for 'em in Salt Lake City,' Petroleum said as he watched them go.

'Ach!' Shoot shrugged. 'They're welcome to it. Let's hope it makes her happy. We've still got our mine, haven't we?'

'We sure have, partner.' Petroleum picked up Korky and swung him round in a jig. 'Let's git back and start diggin'.'

'You know,' Shoot mused later. 'I remember reading in the Bible about Delilah in the Vale of Sorek and how she ruined a man. I never thought to find one like her in the Rocky Mountains.'

'Never ye mind, Shoot,' Petroleum grinned. 'Ye'll recover. Ye'll have a new gal on yer arm in a month or two.'

'Maybe. But I'm never likely to forget Susan Zabriskie.'

ELEVEN

With the execution of the leading lights of the Plummer gang life became more peaceable in Bannack and Virginia, miners and traders being able to go about their business largely unmolested ... or was it a lull before one last storm?

Shoot didn't see a lot of the summer sunshine because he was down the mine with Petroleum hacking out the galena ore, and winching it to the top. Jerry O'Flanagan left his wife and daughter to run his small farm and joined them in the enterprise, and, with a couple of musclemen on the payroll, they were hauling up tons of silver and gold.

'This is one big cow and all we gotta do, gentlemen, is milk it,' Petroleum told them. 'Of course, it ain't gonna be so big as that Comstock lode over in Nevada Territory but it's gonna be big enough.'

'You read about that Eilley Bowers over at the Comstock?' Shoot wiped the grime from his face and took a break for lunch. 'She's built a three hundred thousand dollar mansion in Washoe, brought in three thousand dollar mirrors from Venice, paid a thousand dollars for lace curtains, that's each, and she's just visited London and Paris and run up a bill for a quarter of a million for dresses and jewels. She's spending her ole man, Sandy's, money like water.'

'Durn fool for letting her,' Petroleum said. 'Even a claim like Sandy's won't last for ever.'

'Sure, de woman's crazed with gold,' Jerry remarked in his heavy brogue. 'She'll end in de poorhouse. Mark my words.'*

'I'm putting my share into land and stock,' Shoot told them. 'You need capital to start a big ranch. I don't need no fancy mansion, just a decent-sized house, barns, bunkhouse, corrals and suchlike, but it still costs. Mebbe you can give me a few pointers about land, Jerry?'

'For sure, dere's a choice unclaimed valley jest waitin' t' be used, grass, water, along past Captain Slade's spread. I'm surprised dat greedy bastard hasn't snapped it up.'

'Ach, there's plenty of land in Montana,' Petroleum reminded them. 'But the winters

*This proved to be true. Eilley Bowers ended her days as a penniless fortune-teller.

are too cold here for stock-raising. Me, I'm looking for warmer climes to retire to. I should be able to live in comfort the rest of my life without herding cows.

'I like this big country,' Shoot said. 'It's clean and good. And I've set my heart on ranching and raising a family here.'

'Where you gonna git ya cows from?' one of the other boys chimed in.

'I hear tell some Texan called Chisholm is herding thousands of wild Texas longhorns up through Indian Territ'ry to the railhead at Abilene. Don't see no reason why I can't ride down there, buy a big herd, and drive 'em along the Platte River up to here.'

'It's never been done before.'

'No reason why there shouldn't be a first time.'

'Shoot, I'll be wid ya.' Jerry slapped him on the back. 'And if yese t'inkin' of gittin' wed I got a sweet fifteen-year-old daughter who needs a good man.'

'You don't say?' Shoot grinned, and stretched his back. 'Mebbe I'll have to come to supper at your place one day.'

'Quit ye're dreamin', boys,' Petroleum said, gettin' hold of his pick. 'We got work to do first.'

Captain James Slade had appeared to be a truly converted character and model citizen and, indeed, he was popular with the ladies, who thought him a genial, charming man-of-the-world, and with several leading citizens to whom he had loaned money. As well as ranching and running the Overland Stage he had started a haulage business to transport freight by the new route from Fort Benton with access to the river. In so doing he locked horns with John S. Rockfellow who, more or less, held the monopoly on this sort of thing, and had big merchandising warehouses in Jackson Street, Virginia City, and on the Bannack's Main Street. So, there's nothing wrong with fair competition, but Slade had never been one to play fair.

It was a well-known fact that he had blasted an ounce of shot into a Frenchie called Jules Divine, who ran one of his overland stations at Julesberg. Slade accused the baldpate Divine of selling off his corral of horses for the stage. Jules accused the Sioux of stealing them. Jules was no angel by any means. He didn't get much chance, though, of putting forward a defence. The captain shot him in the back as he was sat one morning at breakfast and watched him slowly die.

It was a way men had in these parts of taking care of business and not a lot was said at the time. But there was a long catalogue of beatings and knifings Slade had been involved in, and it was rumoured he was wanted for killing a man in Illinois.

When he was sober he was very, very jolly. But when he was drunk he could be very, very nasty. And Captain Slade had showed signs of returning to the bottle. He had begun to gather a small band of ruffians about him, of Boon Helm's ilk, of whom there was no shortage in the Territory. He had taken to riding through outlying hamlets and shooting up the town, his favoured trick being to ride his horse into a saloon, douse the lamps with his revolver, and scatter the citizenry.

One late Fall day he rode blatantly into The Golden Garter in Virginia City, well whiskied-up, and tried to feed his horse bottles of champagne. As it was Captain Slade and his boys nobody challenged him, for he always paid for damages when he was off his spree and sobering. But folks were getting mighty tired of it.

Shoot was in the saloon on that particular occasion. He was quenching his thirst, and he watched with interest the captain staggering about, shouting that he rode with the vigilantes that he knew who they were, that they wouldn't dare touch him.

'Uh huh,' Shoot groaned. 'Here we go again.'

He loosened his Colt Navy in his belt and shoved his way out past the pissing horse and his equally pissed owner. On the sidewalk he met the mayor, Jim Castner, and an elderly lawyer, Alexander Davis, who had recently been elected town judge.

'What's happening?' Castner asked.

'Need you ask? The captain's on the rampage again.'

'You can't allow him to terrorize the population like this.' The judge wheezed like a broken harmonium. 'Why don't you arrest him?'

'Why don't you?' Castner asked.

'If you're all too scared, I will,' the old man jutted out his ancient chin. 'I'll write a writ for his arrest for drunkenness and disorderly conduct this minute.'

'Who's gonna present it to him?'

'I will,' the judge said.

They could hear revolvers being shot off, the smashing of glass and a general hullabaloo coming from the saloon as Davis hurried off to his office.

'Something's gotta be done 'bout him,' Castner growled, shoving back his Lincoln hat and wiping his brow with exasperation. 'But that won't work. No jury would convict the captain in this city. Shoot, I've been meaning to ask you. There's a small nucleus of honest men I've enlisted willing to ride as vigilantes again. Would you be their captain?'

'Sorry, Mayor. I'm too busy. Nothing would tempt me. So, he's on a drunk? So what?'

'There's something more serious,' Castner said. 'Ain't you heard about Rockfellow's mule train? The lead mules shot dead, all the freight stolen. Two drivers killed. And that freight, or freight very similar to it, turns up in Captain Slade's new warehouse. Funny, ain't it?'

Shoot stroked his clean-shaven jaw and studied the long, skinny mayor with his steady grey eyes. 'Have you accused him?'

'Have I? You're joking. It would be more than my life's worth.'

'You reckon a vigilante trial's the only way?'

'Sometimes, Shoot, it has to be. Until such time as we get proper law control out here.

We can't back down every time. He's got us all runnin' scared and he knows it.'

Shoot chewed his lip, undecided. He watched the old judge making his arthritic way back to them across Jackson Street from his office waving a piece of paper as if this would guarantee peace in the town. 'He ain't got a chance,' he said. 'There's three desperadoes in there alongside the captain.'

Judge Alexander Davis climbed the sidewalk and headed through the batwing doors of The Golden Garter. 'Come on,' Castner said.

When they pushed into the now dimly lit and shattered remnants of the saloon there was a deathly hush. What few customers and dancing girls were there were backed away in silence watching the judge present the warrant for arrest to Slade.

'What's this?' Slade's face was flushed as he snatched the warrant from Davis. He stood and tore it to shreds. 'Arrest me, would you? You stupid old buzzard. Nobody arrests me in this city.'

The three bodyguards about him had fanned out, their fingers hovering over the butts of their holstered guns, as they grinned, scenting fun to be had.

'I'll take care of this boys.' A two-shot

derringer appeared in the captain's hand from out of his sleeve. He grabbed the judge by the scruff of the neck, pressed the two-inch barrel to his temple, and frogmarched him through Shoot and Castner and out of the swing doors. He swung him a kick to his pants and hurled the old man from the sidewalk into the dust. He stood there hooting with laughter. 'Think yourself lucky I'm lenient, Judge. Anybody else it would be the gunner's daughter.'

Inside, Shoot faced the three thugs, who had ominously cocked their revolvers and had them half-drawn from their belts. He couldn't rely on Jim Castner for support. He licked his lips, nervously. No, the odds weren't too good. 'It ain't my quarrel,' he muttered, and backed out with Castner from the saloon.

Shoot jumped down from the sidewalk to help the old man to his feet, retrieved his hat, and jammed it on his grey hair. 'C'mon, Judge, let's go home,' he said.

He walked away, supporting the old man, towards his office. He heard a yell. John S. Rockfellow had run from his store and was walking determinedly up Jackson with a ten-gauge in his hands. He came to a stop before the smiling and unsteady Slade, and pointed the shot-gun at him. 'If the judge can't arrest you, I will,' he shouted. 'You killed my drivers, stole my freight, Captain. I know that. I'm gonna see you hang.'

He hadn't noticed the derringer in Slade's palm. When he did it was too late. Its deathly little hole was pointed at his eyes. And in a split second its bullet had entered his brain, hurtling him backwards into the dust, his shot-gun discharged harmlessly into the sky.

Shoot's Colt came out in one easy movement as he saw a thug behind Slade draw and aim in his direction. He fired from the hip and the thug pirouetted like a dancer as he was hit, crashing back on to the sidewalk.

Shoot went down on one knee as a second desperado rushed from the saloon, his gun blazing. He was firing wild and the slugs whistled past Shoot's head. Shoot fanned the hammer and fired twice. When the smoke cleared he saw the man leaning back against the saloon's clapboard wall, blood blossoming on his shirt, as he slowly slid down into a repose of death.

The captain had fired his second shot into the body of Rockfellow, and was out of lead. Realizing this, he slowly raised his hand and, in a muddled, maudlin way, muttered,

'What's happening, boys?'

Shoot cocked his Colt waiting for the third man, some lowlife known as Bill Hunter. There was a thud of horse's hooves. Hunter came hurtling out from the back of the saloon, charged away up Jackson Street and out of town.

'Where you going, Bill?' the captain called plaintively, looking after him.

'What shall we do with him?' Castner asked. 'Hang him now?'

'No.' Judge Davis waggled his finger at the mayor. 'He'll get a proper trial tomorrow. Then we'll hang him. Put him in the lock-up.'

'You can't be serious, boys?' Slade wheedled out expressions of fondness for them as Shoot and Castner got hold of him. 'You saw it was self-defence. He was going to *kill* me.'

'We'll see what the jury thinks about that in the morning.' Castner accompanied them up the road, unlocked a sturdy cabin with barred windows, and shoved Slade into it in spite of his protests. 'People have had enough of you, Captain. Maybe now we'll get a little peace around here at nights.'

TWELVE

He was tied up in the boughs of a tree, a longarm pressed to his shoulder. He could see the grey-clad Rebs creeping through the wood beneath him. There was a scatter of grapeshot and he was falling, crashing to the ground. He was held helpless by the tree as a Reb reared over him, his bayonet poised to plunge. Shoot heard the screams and shouts about him and saw the man's face, a grinning half-shot-away skull, his grey uniform in tatters over strips of bloody flesh. He was laughing horribly, welcoming him to hell...

Shoot broke from the dream with a start, sitting up, sweat pouring from him although the room was cold. He had thought he had escaped from the nightmares of the war. Would they always pursue him? The memories of the stench, the death, the fear? Or was it the killing of the two men yesterday had brought it all back? He got no kick of power, like some did, from taking life. Where was he? Hadn't he heard a gunshot? Or was that in the dream?

He rolled out of bed and opened the curtains. It was already grey daylight, the first thin fall of frosty snow glittering on the roads, rooftops and windows. He had taken a room above Castner's Idaho Restaurant. He had come to Virginia City to arrange for some big ore-crushing equipment to be freighted in. There was something going on down there. People shouting, men carrying someone between them. It was a body, the arms hanging down limp, the clothing bloody. It was Jim Castner's son, Luke!

'I sent him across with some coffee for Slade. I shoulda gone myself.' The mayor was staring through distraught eyes at his sixteen-year-old boy laid out on one of the tables of the restaurant. 'Bill Hunter was waiting. He knifed him, cut his insides out. He didn't need to do that. He took his keys, set Slade free.'

'Luke never hurt anyone.' Mrs Castner was stroking her son's face as if trying to coax him back to life. Tears were streaming from her eyes. She looked up at Shoot through their blur, and gave a scream of agony. 'Why should he do that?'

'What was that gunshot?'

'Barney Hughes took a pot at 'em as they

rode outa town,' the drugstore owner, Zachary Clare, said. 'It's a damned shame. We shoulda done it yesterday.'

The men and women standing around nodded dumbly, or murmured in agreement. They all knew what he meant. Some turned their eyes on Shoot. His fast-shooting of the day before had been told around the town. They needed somebody to lead them.

'We'd like to be alone with our grief,' the mayor said, and the folk began to file out of the restaurant. 'Shoot!' he called. 'Can I have a word with you?'

When they had all gone Castner said, 'About that job I offered you?'

Shoot met his eyes and nodded, gravely. 'I'll lead 'em.'

'You know what to do?'

Shoot spun the cylinder of his revolver. 'I know what to do. Mad dogs gotta be put down, ain't they?'

'I'll try to rustle up the boys. Most of them are out of town, at their mines and ranches. There's others still won't want to go against the captain.'

'I'd like to git goin' straight away,' Shoot said. 'While their tracks are still fresh in this snow.'

'Molly,' Castner shouted to his serving girl. 'Get Shoot some breakfast, steak and eggs. And fix him hard-tack rations for two days. I'll go see who I can find. I'll tell 'em to meet you outa town under the Murderer's Tree in an hour. We don't want everyone to know who you are. I'll ride with you.'

'There's no need for you to come, Jim. We'll take care of it. Or die tryin'.'

Shoot was surprised to see the druggist, Zachary, a somewhat dandified young man, still wearing his four-button suit, derby, and fur coat, among the five men waiting for him beneath the former gallows. And Buck Beechey, who ran the gunshop, and was loaded with his own weaponry. The others looked more dependable, square-jawed, straight-eyed men, a rancher and his two hands.

They did not speak, but spurred their horses away to seek Slade and Hunter's trail. 'Looks like they're headed for the Gallantin River country,' one said.

They rode at a steady lope all day under a pewter-grey sky. Shoot had strapped on his two revolvers and had his carbine in the saddle boot. He had buttoned his reefer jacket high against the bitter wind and, with a red bandanna, his low-crowned hat, leather shot-gun chaps protecting his legs, boots and spurs, there was little to distinguish him now from any ranch hand. His spirit had been forged in the fire of war, and tempered by his love or lust for the money-hungry Susan. He rode before them with a calm, icy determination.

A severe snowstorm enveloped them in the afternoon, blotting out the trail, but they rode on, reckoning that the fugitives were aiming to cross the big mountains between the Stinkingwater and the Madison. They forded the Madison with some difficulty for it was already beginning to ice over, which cut into the horses' flanks as they floundered through the strong currents. When night came they ground-hitched the horses, gave them some corn, built a fire, brewed up coffee, and chewed on jerky.

'Seems to me they tryin' to git right outa the Territ'ry,' one of the ranch boys drawled as he rolled some Bull Durham. 'Slade must know he's all played out here in Montana.'

'Jim said he'd emptied the contents of his safe,' Zachary muttered. 'So it seems like it.'

They lay down on the frozen earth with no shelter but their blankets wrapped around them. Shoot pulled his seaman's woollen hat down across his nose and ears against the frostbite and wriggled fully-clothed into his tarp sack. He managed some shut-eye in spite of the intense cold.

In the middle of the night a wild yell awoke them all. Young Zachary had lain on top of a hillock as close as he could to the fire. He had rolled over and landed in the middle of it. He was jumping about dusting the burning cinders off his fine singed suit. He had changed his position with marvellous rapidity.

This little incident gave the other men much amusement, and seemed to buoy up their spirits. At dawn they saddled up and set off at a brisk pace. The weather had changed very much for the worse, a fierce snowstorm, driven by a furious wind, blowing full in their faces. Not one spoke of abandoning their mission. They gritted their teeth, pulled hats down over eyes, and ploughed on.

'At least they won't be able to see us coming,' the rancher said when, mid-morning, they paused to cook up a mountaineer's breakfast. 'That might be a good thing. He's handy with a rifle is Hunter.'

'As well as a knife,' Shoot said, as they

crouched, trying to warm their frozen hands, collars turned up against the tempest.

They pushed on, hour after hour until, about six o'clock as the light was beginning to fade, the low timber buildings of the Milk Ranch hove into view. They approached with caution in case Slade had taken up habitation. The owner, Jeremiah Temple, thrust a rifle out of a window and called, 'What you buzzards want?'

Shoot rode forward, raised a hand, and shouted, 'We're the Vigilante Committee. We're after Cap'n Slade. Has he passed this way?'

'He sure has,' Temple said, as he came out on the porch. 'Him and some *hombre* were very abusive to me and my wife. They took fresh horses and supplies. Lit outa here about two hours ago.'

The exhausted riders looked at each other. They were hungry and cold but maybe it would be best to carry on?

'Come on in, boys,' Temple said. 'Warm your bones and have supper.'

It was too welcome an offer to refuse. They feasted on fresh bread and beef stew around a blazing fire and gave an account of Slade's crimes and misdemeanours to Temple.

'He's a fine-soundin' gentleman but he certainly didn't endear hisself to me,' the rancher drawled. 'Said he'd havta owe me for the hosses. My best stock. I didn't feel like arguin' with that evil-faced fella with him.'

Mr Temple insisted they have fresh horses, so an hour or so later, warmed and refreshed, they saddled up and set off into the darkness across the gleaming snow. The moon had risen and they could see the clear indentations of the outlaws' trail.

At about midnight they saw the glow of a camp fire in a cover of pines. 'I reckon that's them,' Zachary said.

'We gotta be sure,' Shoot replied. 'It could be a coupla miners. We don't want no accidents on this picnic.'

They dismounted, tethered their horses, took off their gauntlets, blew on their fingers, and drew their revolvers. They set off in different directions to encircle the camp.

Shoot could see two shadowy figures rolled in blankets beside the fire. They didn't seem to be keeping any guard. He stepped out and approached through the brush. The crack of a twig made one of the men leap up. He had a rifle in his hands. It was Bill Hunter. There was an explosion. A slug whistled past Shoot's ear. He ran in, thrust the rifle aside with one arm and crashed his right fist into Hunter's jaw. He followed up with a boot in his groin to make sure. Hunter fell back on to the fire, groaning.

The other vigilantes ran from the shadows and collared Slade, who was fumbling for his revolver. He did not argue when he saw four similar Colt .45s cocked and aimed at him.

'Howdy, boys,' the captain said. 'How on earth did you get here?' He seemed genuinely surprised to see them.

'Howdja think?' Zachary snarled, and grabbed him by his tie, his fist raised. 'By some hard ridin' after you bastards.'

'Hold it, Zach,' Buck said. 'No need for that. We have another remedy.'

'Just a minute,' Shoot butted in, nursing his fingers. 'I figure on takin' 'em back for trial.'

'Not again.' Zachary spat in the snow with disgust. 'We've had enough of trials. This guy's got friends. What about Luke Castner with his guts cut out? Think of that.'

'Boys.' Captain Slade had risen and was trying to be bluffingly genial. 'That was nothing to do with me. It was Bill here. I told him it was an awful unnecessary thing to do. You'll never stick that on me.'

'You're as guilty as him. If not more guilty. You've had the advantages he ain't. You've thrown your life away, Slade.'

'Don't be fools, boys.' For the first time a spasm of fear seemed to come into the captain's eyes, like a steer sensing the slaughter yards. 'I've got gold in those saddle-bags. A fortune. It's all yours. I'm leaving Montana. Just let me go. Or take me back to Virginia City.'

The rancher was calmly kneeling brewing up coffee on the fire, casting a careful glance at Hunter, who was sitting whimpering to himself. He had been sure to relieve him of his hunting knife. He passed round a tin mug of steaming brew to the men.

'That pine,' one of the cowhands mused. 'It seems to have been fashioned by nature for the job.'

A horizontal limb at a convenient height was there for the rope. On the trunk was a spur like a belaying pin on which to fasten the end. He strode over, took a coil of hemp lariat from the saddle horn of one of the horses. He sent it snaking over the bough. 'We can even use their own rope.'

'You know my feelings. I'm against this sort of thing,' Shoot said. 'But I'll abide by the majority decision. OK. Those in favour of hanging go to the far side of the fire.'

Four men stepped across the ashes and turned to face him, their eyes determined. 'So be it,' Shoot muttered.

'You can't be serious.' Slade's face had gone as white as the snow. 'At least give me a few days to settle my affairs.'

Hunter made a bolt for it, but they grabbed him, hauled him back at gunpoint and made him climb on a horse. Buck fashioned a sturdy noose and placed it round his neck. Hunter's eyes bulged. 'I'll see you in hell, Cap'n,' he shouted. Each whipped the horse's haunches and it bolted away. The rope twanged taut and Bill Hunter swung suspended, his legs kicking, his hands flailing desperately at his throat.

It took him a few seconds to die. Buck jerked on his boots to make sure. 'That must be the first truthful thing he's said for many a year, Captain. Are you next?'

Slade had begun to shake violently. 'Give me a drink,' he gasped, his voice sounding strangled.

Maybe it was delirium tremens. Maybe not.

Shoot handed him his flask of whiskey. 'Maybe if you hadn't had so much of that pizen you wouldn't be in this spot now.'

The captain emptied the flask down his gulping throat, which brought a little colour back to his cheeks. He took a deep breath. 'I'm ready. Will you help me on to my horse?' He had gone as weak as a kitten and they had to haul him up, fix the noose around his neck. He took a look at the distorted face of Hunter swinging nearby, crossed himself and appeared to mouth a prayer. 'Go ahead, boys, I've only myself to blame. You're on a good undertaking.'

Shoot, himself, slapped the horse's haunches this time, and launched James Slade into Eternity.

As he stood and watched the two miscreants hanging there, somehow peaceful-looking in the silent, slowly falling snowflakes, a sense of awe at life's narrow tightrope, and relief that the chase was over came over him.

'The ground's too durn hard to bury them,' the rancher growled.

'Leave 'em for the buzzards,' Zachary said.

'No,' Shoot replied. 'We'll cut 'em down, load 'em on the horses, take 'em back.'

As luck had it, when they got back to Virginia City, a lawman called West was waiting. He had ridden four hundred miles from Illinois with a warrant for the arrest of Slade, dead or alive.

'You can have him with pleasure,' Shoot said.

In the days that followed, when he wasn't working down the mine he became a frequent visitor at O'Flanagan's farm. When he first set eyes on Mary she was coming out of the barn with two buckets of milk held by a yoke across her sturdy shoulders. She trudged across the mud-churned yard, her dark hair hanging in disorder from a mob cap, a streak of mud on her nose. She froze in her tracks when she saw Shoot.

'Howdy,' he drawled. She sure was a pretty thing, a fresh-faced country girl, pert breasts pushing out her cotton pinafore. 'My name's Johannson.'

'I know.' She looked up at him on his horse. 'I've heard a lot about you. I feel like I already know you .

He jumped down and helped her in with the pails. And, in spite of the cow muck on her boots, she smelt good and warm and female and he knew she was the one for him.

One night after supper they stepped outside to take a look at the stars, or so they said.

'Tell me,' Shoot said, as he pulled her alongside the cabin and stood over her. 'Are you the sort of gal who'd like to go to Paris and spend two hundred thousand dollars on dresses and jewels and mirrors for some crazy mansion?'

'No I ain't.' She hooked her arms around his neck and kissed him. 'I'm happy as I am, 'long as I got you.'

'And iffen I went off with your ole man to Kansas and was away a long time, would you wait for me?'

'I'd be here when you got back, doncha worry.'

'You wouldn't go off with some ole doctor man?'

'Why should I do that?' She giggled and pressed her body into him. 'That would be a fool thing to do.'

'And you don't jest like me 'cause I got money in the bank?'

'You're a good man, Shoot. Pa was right about that. I'd love ya if ya didn' have a cent.'

Her nose was chill against his, and her lips soft and yielding. She had the same green eyes as Susan, but she had none of her haughtiness. Her hair was thickly black and Irish, but fell about her face in a tangle. And her face was pert and girlish. This was the way love ought to be, he thought. Fun. Not torment.

'You sure look pretty in the moonlight,' he whispered, and he was undoing her blouse, feeling for her breasts.

'Shoot. No!' She wriggled to evade him, and gave a shrill squawk as she slipped, and they went tumbling down to land in deep snow in a ditch. She lay and looked up at him. 'We mustn't,' she breathed. But she knew that they would. He was pulling up her dress and easing her pantalets off over her boots, and fumbling at his own clothes. And then it was as if they were possessed, thrashing and gasping in the snow.

'Wow!' she said afterwards, as he lay upon her, breathing hard. 'I never knew it was gonna be like that. You'll have to get off, Shoot, my bottom's frozen.'

'So are my danged balls.'

He felt her body quivering beneath him, and saw that she was laughing, helplessly. He began snorting with laughter himself, as he sat up and began pulling up his pants.

Suddenly the cabin door opened and Jerry O'Flanagan stood there over them, a shotgun in his hands.

'What in tarnation's going on out here?' he demanded.

He took in the situation and bellowed, 'Daughter, what d'ye t'ink ye're doin'? Haven't I taught ye Irish hospitality? Dat boy's likely to catch de pneumonia.

As Shoot and Mary grinned at each other and, sheepishly, when they were decent, followed O'Flanagan back into the cabin, Jerry growled at his wife, 'Mother, I tink it's time dese two was wedded.'

And so, a week later, they were.

AFTERWORD

This story was based on true events that occurred in Montana Territory in the lawless years of 1862–63 when twenty-six men were hanged by the Vigilante Committee. These included Captain James Slade, Marshal Henry Plummer, Boon Helm, Gad Moore, Cyrus Skinner, Robert Zachary and Bill Hunter. Among several others banished were Judge Cyril Smith and 'Parsnip' Sessions for circulating bogus gold. In 1873 the *San Francisco Times* recorded the case of Susan Zabriskie accused of poisoning her wealthy doctor husband. She was hanged.

The publishers hope that this book has given you enjoyable reading. Large Print Books are especially designed to be as easy to see and hold as possible. If you wish a complete list of our books please ask at your local library or write directly to:

Dales Large Print Books
Magna House, Long Preston,
Skipton, North Yorkshire.
BD23 4ND

This Large Print Book for people
who cannot read normal print
is published under the auspices of

THE ULVERSCROFT FOUNDATION

[illegible] you have enjoyed this Book.
Please think for a moment about those
who have worse eyesight than you ...
and are unable to even read or enjoy
Large Print, without great difficulty.

You can help them by sending a
donation, large or small to:

The Ulverscroft Foundation,
1, The Green, Bradgate Road,
Anstey, Leicestershire, LE7 7FU,
England.

or request a copy of our brochure for
more details.

The Foundation will use all donations
to assist those people who are visually
impaired and need special attention
with medical research, diagnosis
and treatment.

Thank you very much for your help.